A Rude Awakening

Edward J. Herdrich

This book is for:

Linda B. – *promises to keep.*

My editor – *for your inspiration and perspiration, both of which made this book possible.*

Contents

PROLOGUE
Sunday, May 29th
9:15 p.m.

"This ain't fucking *Johnny Dangerously* or something, you moron," Vito yelled at Tony as they walked to the back of the warehouse.

"Yeah, no shit, Sherlock," Tony responded and flicked his cigarette butt at Vito.

"You two clowns want to stop that shit right now?" Michael asked, stepping over and standing in front of the two men who were taller than he was. He looked from one to the other, staring unflinchingly. Unlike Fred, who knew enough to keep his weapon invisible without a full body search, Vito and Tony sometimes seemed to have walked straight out of a mail order thug catalogue best exemplified by Wilmer in the *Maltese Falcon*, their firearms thinly veiled by their jackets. Michael doubted that either one of them had ever seen the movie. "Now follow me."

"What's he want to talk to us about anyways, Michael?" Vito asked.

"He doesn't want to talk to you. He wants to talk to me. Then, I'll tell you what needs to be done. Any more questions?"

"So then why'd we have to come down here?" Tony asked.

Michael closed his eyes for a moment, inhaled and exhaled deeply. "Did you actually see *Johnny Dangerously*, Vito? Huh? Tell me, what did you think?"

"It wasn't so good...stuff like that don't happen."

"Very good, brain trust. No, it doesn't," Michael sighed. "The movie was a spoof. A satire. If you ever feel like

4

a second career, don't look for a job as a movie critic, if you couldn't figure that out."

"It was a comedy?"

"Okay, forget it. Here's all you need to remember about movies. Comedy and tragedy. Ready? Comedy is when bad shit happens to you, tragedy is when it happens to me."

They stopped outside a door marked "Shipping and Receiving." Through smoked glass, they could see three figures inside, one seated behind a desk, the other two standing. They couldn't hear any conversation coming from the room. Michael knocked twice, and one of the standing men opened the door. Only Michael stepped inside.

"Don Justino," Michael said and stepped forward to the desk. He bowed his head for a moment and then looked back up. "I'm honored."

"Michael, it's good to see you," Don Justino said and motioned for Michael to sit. "You know, I will be heading back to the old country soon. My health is not so good lately. But, there are a few things that I need taken care of before I go. I know I can trust you."

"Thank you, sir. I do my best for the family."

"I know. And you've earned a place, but that is not a talk for right now. This is important to me. You know Fred Batiste, right?"

"Uh, yes," Michael replied, his voice slightly wavering.

"Michael, relax. Just because of what Fred does for us doesn't mean we only talk to people about Fred if they're on his list. I like you, Michael. I need your brains and talent on this."

"Thank you, sir. What can I do?"

"Fred is special to me. I don't want him taken out by his replacement, like so many specialists before him. I have no worries with Fred. So, I want to throw Fred a retirement party, for real. I need you to talk to the city and the police. I want a nice place, but private and safe. I want good food and music. And, I want this girl, the one in these ads, at the party. Whether or not Fred walks out with her, no one knows. But I know this is the kind of girl he likes. Find out who she is, whether or not she's married. Do it only through the safe channels."

Michael picked up the two ads from the desktop, one for perfume, the other for a band. The perfume ad featured a very attractive young woman, wearing blue jeans and flannel, laughing at something the pretty boy beside her with the fishing pole must have said—as if either one of them had ever been fishing at a remote lake. The ad for the band looked as if they had pulled a still from a video, and no one was really trying to hide the fact it was little more than soft porn. Her skin was a creamy chocolate, and her hair was not straightened as in the other ad, more strongly revealing she was biracial. Her hair was long and tightly curled but in a manner that looked like it could have come from either side of her family. She did not look the unhealthy skinny of most models.

"Does she know anything?"

"No. You talk to the people who talk to her handlers. Keep our influence invisible to her. I just want her there, no muscle, no tricks. And, outside this room, nobody knows about her. I want it so as far as she knows, she is just there for a party that could be important for her career. If Fred makes something happen, okay. He doesn't like working girls anyway. He'll be moving a day or two after the party—he's smart enough to know that if he gets to retire, it's still on our terms. You understand?"

"Yes, sir." Michael nodded. It was unusual, but clear. She should go there knowing nothing and walk away knowing nothing other than what Fred might tell her. The people at this party would not be talking business. Even with the police and city saying it would be a hands-off night, that just meant no warrants would be served; it didn't mean audio and video wouldn't be rolling. If Fred couldn't get her attention, that would be okay too. He'd be moving soon and happy to be able to do whatever he wanted. Probably open a small business. Maybe a restaurant.

"You can do this for me in six weeks or less?"

"Sir, that is plenty of time. But, Don Justino, I am leaving tomorrow to California to take care of some other business. Can it wait two weeks for me to start?"

"Yes. Okay, good," Don Justino replied, sat back in his chair, and smiled. "How's your family, Michael? Theresa, she's happy? Good. Your little girl is in college next year? Good, maybe she'll go into law school, eh?"

Michael laughed, nodded, and hugged as was appropriate under the circumstances. He stepped out, turned to face the open warehouse area, and slowly pressed the door closed. It would cost some money to keep the police and city away, but they always needed money. He knew he needed someone with finesse to find the girl without setting off alarms. Tony and Vito were good for collections and corrections and always made people think twice if they didn't like what Michael had to tell them. They were only good for back up here, though. Sometimes they were best left waiting in the car.

Music and movies, Michael thought, motioning for Tony and Vito to follow him as he walked toward the exit. Alligator and Delmark were the first two record labels that came to mind, but he knew there were others. Chess was out of business, their building on South Michigan now home to a Blues Heaven Foundation, whatever that was. All the punk and indie labels, Michael knew, he would have to rely on other people to handle. Wasn't there an attorney in the business that owed the family a favor?

"So," Vito asked as Michael stopped at the doorway.

"You gonna maybe tell us somethin'?"

"Once upon a time..." Michael joked and opened the door to the outside, glad to feel the cool breeze in his face. "Look, guys, I'm not sure why you had to be here. I'm tired, you're tired. We'll talk in the morning, after some sleep."

Michael looked at both of them. They both nodded their consent. They were good soldiers. Not the brightest bulbs, but not the dullest either. There wouldn't be much for them to do on this assignment, so Michael assumed that they had been asked to come with more as protection than anything else. It was part of Don Justino's ways.

Michael was almost relieved that Don Justino would be leaving for the old country soon. He was easy to work for, simple and direct most of the time. Even when he would talk about history, politics, and all the larger subjects around their business, he wasn't hard to follow. But his nostalgia for the old ways of the Chicago-style mafia that went out in the 20th century could be tiresome. Most of the families and their organizations had moved into the 21st century, all of their business behind legitimate companies or in the world of lobbyists. Don Justino, though, still liked to have meetings in warehouses and other nostalgic moments.

This assignment shouldn't be too difficult though, Michael thought. After all, it wasn't like anyone would mess with Fred. And if the girl was getting known in the industry, she shouldn't be too hard to find. Time was not a pressing matter, for a change. He had been given six weeks, and it probably wouldn't take more than two or three. Michael nodded to Tony for opening the car door, got in the back seat, sat back, and closed his eyes. Something simple for a change.

CHAPTER ONE

Sunday, June 16th
1:15 a.m.

He felt and saw his legs moving, but he did not move forward. It was as if the force he generated was met immediately by an invisible, intangible...something. Not like something pushing against him, but rather that his motions occurred with no effect. Silence enveloped and blanketed him, almost like he just entered a vacuum, but at the same time there was a rumbling crash. He felt it would be similar to being in a soundproof tunnel under the stage at a rock concert—he could feel the sound waves but not hear anything.

Dressed in a double-breasted, pin-striped suit of a non-descript color, he couldn't move his torso except in a twisting motion. He was...nowhere. A lack of color or detail surrounded him, denying both place and time. He tried to scream. The sound echoed and reverberated in his head, but he didn't know if anything had actually come out of his mouth. Slowly, the whitewashed, blank emptiness crept forward and covered him, and it brought with it a new and strong fear that the nothingness was temporary.

It was. Suddenly, they were getting closer. Just faces at first, then people. Appearing at first as pasty as the background, they each seemed vaguely familiar to him, yet he felt he didn't really know any of them. They moved effortlessly, gliding more than walking. Now, they were all in color. Bright red splashed over blues, greens, and yellows. He was in black and white, suffocating.

"Every dog has his day, Fred. Every dog has his day," he heard. It was unmistakably the voice of Sam Carlini, only

now in a somehow sinister, almost tin-can, echoing wave of sound. Sam had gotten him introductions and even trained him a little, and then was his first assignment. Only, Sam was not one of the faces approaching.

The faces changed and came together in a swirling, movie-like quickness. Now there was only one: a wire-haired terrier, its mouth opening wider, its impossibly long incisors glistening.

Fred O. Batiste rolled off his bed, his head knocking the leg of the nest tables. His hands stopped his fall, instinct taking over even in his groggy state. He squeezed his eyes tight for a moment and then slowly, lifting his head a little bit, opened them up.

"Jesus fucking Chr—" Fred said aloud. "Sorry, I didn't mean that. But, what the hell was that?"

He scanned the room. He was still outside himself, feeling a dull wave of fear and loss, to a certain degree, because of that feeling. As soon as he heard the sound of his own voice, he knew the answer to his question; it had been a nightmare. For a lot of people, that would have made the fear dissipate. For Fred, that realization only brought a different kind of fear.

He had not had a nightmare since he was seven.

He had known sensible, reasonable fear all his life. You were afraid of the Don being displeased with you. You were afraid of leaving any clues for the Feds. You were afraid of some weak link rolling over. And, if you were smart, you were afraid of the day you became your replacement's first assignment. But this nightmare was not a sensible fear. And for Fred, that was worse.

As an enforcement specialist for the Don, it was part of his job to make sure nothing shook him out of his routine, nothing caused him to act out of character. This nightmare had come from years ago, from when he was a child growing up in Melrose Park, and the terrier that had scared him. Fred had taken care of the dog the next day with the advice and aid of Sam Carlini and a plate of tainted manicotti.

Sam, who was revered as the best enforcer any of the Chicago families had known, had disappeared as Fred was just starting his career. Sam taught Fred many things, from little things like that the word *hitman* was an outdated term, to the more important things, like the fact he and Fred were among the most expendable of family.

"This is important, Fred," Sam had said in his gently-commanding, tenor voice. "You got to keep some things for yourself, be more than your job—and always watch your back. Maybe it's another family going to get you, maybe one of your own orders your termination."

Those were some of the last words he heard from Sam over twenty years ago. Sam disappeared a few months before Fred was ordered to take him out. Fred was never sure if he understood exactly what Sam meant. Sam was always reading books on just about everything from law to philosophy to psychology. Twice when Sam had taken him to meet Don Justino, he had listened to them talk at length about those things. As far as Fred knew Sam never let anyone else know about his reading.

Now though, here in Franklin Park years later, something had triggered that memory. Something was making him nervous for the first time since he had been in grade school. His drinking was the obvious answer, but somewhere, something else had been added. He hadn't thought of Sam in years, and Fred would be surprised if he were still alive. So why was he having a nightmare with Sam in it now? Except for the pictures Don Justino kept of Sam and his daughter, nothing brought Sam to his conscious mind.

"Where the hell am I?" Fred paused again, took in another scan of the room. "Oh shit, I'm in my fucking bedroom."

He reached up with a shaky hand to grab the water glass on the nightstand. He gulped down the contents of the glass, feeling the warm, thick, mellow burn of sipping whiskey on his throat, and smiled. He stood up, and then he saw the woman. The smile faded.

She was lying on the bed, curled up underneath the comforter and slate gray silk sheets, her face turned the other direction. All he could see was her long, curly, strikingly dark brown hair.

"Who are you?" he said quietly, more to himself than to the still body, his weak, wavering hand reaching to the back of his neck. "I hope it was good for you, cuz I don't remember nothin'."

In his disturbed and distracted state, he could only think of getting a real drink. He looked around the room, his eyes squinting as they crossed to the lamp lit on the small table near the bathroom. The bathroom. He really needed the bathroom more than he needed a drink.

He stumbled across the room and into the master bathroom. Master f-ing bathroom, he thought. As if anybody needed a whirlpool bath and a freaking shower room the size of a small bedroom. But, the remodel had been a gift. And, want it or not, gifts from certain people you accept willingly, with gratitude and apparent enthusiasm.

"Jesus f—sorry, sorry," he said. He zipped up and started to leave the bathroom when he caught his reflection in the mirror and was taken aback by the face staring back at him. Could drinking really add that many years that quickly?

He was still not showing many of the outward signs of being in his fifties. His chestnut brown hair was showing no signs of gray, and there were no furrows in his brow or lines on his forehead, no loose flesh on his neck. His eyes, though, seemed somehow sunken, and his skin had a dull roughness to it he was certain was a recent development. There was no denying his workouts were getting harder to recover from; he was seeing the aging for the first time.

"Now I really need that drink," he said and thought better than to flush because he didn't want to wake his sleeping visitor. He wasn't quite ready to talk to her yet.

He walked down the stairs, past the main floor, and down to the expansive finished basement. The black leather couch and chrome and smoked-glass table reflected the same sense of stylishly bland decorating as the prints on the wall. A print of Italy, showing a montage of an open market with a withered woman selling peppers and an old man tossing pizza dough in the window of a restaurant, hung next to an equally generic photo of the Chicago skyline. Like all the prints, they seemed as if they could have been bought in a print shop in any mall, even their frames screaming of production line.

Fred ran his hand along the covered pool table. Apparently, they hadn't knocked any balls around besides his. He smiled, feeling a little clearer as he approached the bar. He had bought the table more for guests; it was a tradition, like something you should have in your house when it was this nice. He liked to play every once in a while, but the shallow imprints in the chalk reflected the fact that it wasn't even close to a hobby.

His eyes fixed on the open, unlabeled bottle of whiskey in the center of the table. Whomever she was, he had wanted to impress her. The whiskey was one of three bottles he was given for his 40th birthday from Jimmy, the only person he trusted to work on his cars. Jimmy's brother still made it in very small, painstaking batches. Only a select few got to experience the results.

He reached for the whiskey and, grabbing it tightly, debated for a second about drinking it straight from the bottle. He reconsidered and, without looking, reached over the black marble countertop to the shelf below and grabbed a glass. He poured a double shot and slammed it back. He let the warmth hit his stomach and spread throughout his body. Now that the edge was off, he poured a glass to sip slowly and enjoy. He set the glass down on the bar, a slight series of clinks as the teetering glass settled.

"For Christ's sake...oops, forget I said that," Fred said aloud. "Good thing I ain't a sniper. Man, that ain't even funny—something's gotta break."

He took a slow sip and looked up at the clock. The left arm of Frank Sinatra pointed at one, the right at six, as Frankie strolled down a city street. He remembered the woman upstairs.

"Hell, it's only one-thirty," he said and turned around. "Maybe she's not too deeply into that sleep."

Glass in hand, Fred walked slowly up the stairs and approached the old world, hand crafted door. He knocked gently before walking in. He looked around the room, unsure of the last few weeks and needing to admire the room where he kept his most private possessions. The collection of art, furniture, and curios from various cultures eased his nerves a little more. His eyes were drawn to a framed picture caught at the periphery of his vision, a picture of a little Korean girl and her brother walking down the road holding hands, an ox-drawn cart beside them, a light rain falling.

He had gone to their village to watch his assignment in Korea get to visit his grandmother. Fred had called on the grandmother under the pretext of being interested in some of the furniture she was known to sell—he had to determine if she was at all involved in the smuggling operation. It took only light conversation and brief observations to know she wasn't. That had been an easy assignment. Her grandson was known to be a somewhat reckless surfer, so the accident didn't surprise anyone. There were many reasons a surfer's board might not be found after a fatal accident, from being swept away by the tides to being destroyed in the accident.

He had known immediately he needed the picture he had taken on the way there. The pictures had become like Sam's reading. He couldn't exactly explain it, but there was something about a certain kind of photography that he enjoyed. Photographs captured more than just the objects themselves. Before he left, he went back and bought the set of nesting tables the old lady had talked to him about, feigning ignorance and overpaying as if he were an ordinary tourist.

He never even tried to find out who the boy and girl were that he captured in the photograph. It wasn't important. That picture gave him a different sense of almost melancholic nostalgia than the one just below it from his Paris assignment, the old French couple holding hands and sharing an upward look at the Eiffel Tower. But both left him with a sense of pride at a moment, a mood, maybe even something more captured.

He had been down on Polk street, just off Taylor, taking pictures of and around Fontano's—pictures he had thought the Don might like—when someone told him about the party. It was not supposed to be a family party, and that made it more appealing to Fred. Sometimes Fred enjoyed being where no one knew him. Somewhere where people were not either avoiding him or trying to determine who he was within the family.

He took another sip of whiskey, holding the liquid in his mouth for a moment, savoring the flavor. These pictures, framed and bordered with an eye for detail and color, were not like most of the flat, dull, factual pictures he took for his assignments. Those pictures, most of which were destroyed along with their negatives soon after they were reviewed, spoke of necessary details and verifications. His private pictures, he often joked, were not some Ansel Adams over-sized postcard crap. He never really told anyone what exactly they were, and sometimes he even wondered why he had started taking them.

Almost everyone, even some the people who thought they knew him, seemed to believe he couldn't appreciate people outside the family or beyond assignments. The Don, who had known Sam better than anyone, knew about the pictures and understood. Meeting people and learning about how they lived, Fred thought, was something hardly anyone ever put together with his line of work. Hell, it was even interesting listening to some of the non-Christian religious beliefs. Like people who talked about hauntings and aliens— interesting, even if completely ridiculous.

He took another sip of whiskey and turned his attention to his guest. Her hair was a deep, dark mahogany, and long. The partial profile revealed young, smooth, whipped-milk-chocolate colored skin. He looked at her lying on her side, her figure roughly outlined in the gray-blue blanket, and wondered when the last time was he came home with a woman. He didn't have anything to do with professionals. Most of them were headcases still suffering the effects of abuse. If not, they were women who didn't have enough respect for themselves to at least use their body for big money. Either way, they couldn't be trusted.

"You must have really tied one on," he said and sat slowly, softly, down on the bed so as not to startle her. The humor in his voice faded as he noticed that when he shifted his weight to move toward her, the motion caused her body to pitch slightly, then loll back in an inanimate fashion. The skin on her cheeks was an underlying ashen color. He touched her shoulder under the covers, and he recognized the coolness. He closed his eyes for a minute, letting out a sigh.

He opened his eyes, sat up, and moved a bit closer. He grabbed her chin, turning her head. There was a small bullet hole in the middle of her forehead with a small drop of dried blood. He turned her head again. In her left ear, two earrings; in her right, none. He opened her mouth, looking back to the molars. Number 32 was missing.

"Oh Christ, oh Jesus fuck...sorry, didn't mean that. Son of a bitch. When did I fucking do this? Did I do this? I can't remember doing this. I don't even remember bringing her home." He scanned the bed for any signs of blood or personal items. He looked around at the area immediately surrounding the bed. Though he hadn't had to do any of his own clean-up work in years, it was as instinctual as any other task learned through repetition and meticulous attention. He looked back at the woman. It appeared to be his signature work, except one of the first rules was that you never bring an assignment to any address associated with you or them—witness potential was too high.

His scan expanded to the rest of the room. Clothing, jewelry, purse, anything that might belong to her. His conscious mind directed his self-preservation actions, which were necessary. His mind was now on auto-pilot, and reality was hitting hard. He had to make her completely disappear. The part of the job he had been glad to leave behind as he gained status, but not something you ever forgot about. *If there are no witnesses, and they don't have a body, it will be a while before they investigate it as a homicide.*

His unconscious mind was moving faster, trying to answer all the questions that arose from no memory of the last six hours. He was having trouble with just accepting it was six hours gone. Could being clean and sober for only three months cause a little slide to lead to this? Was this somebody setting him up? Who? His replacement? Had this girl been at the party? Did he meet her somewhere else? Did anyone see them together? Who had driven? No matter what, he needed to talk to his sponsor on Monday about the slip and getting back on track. Finding that person to admit the exact nature of his wrongs to was still a struggle.

More immediate concerns first, he thought. He took a couple of pictures with his phone. Phones were great. The picture lasted as long as you wanted it to; then, you just tossed the phone. He started to make his way to the basement to assess his cleaning supplies. Did he have a set of knives and cutting tools that would do the job? It would be a good six hours of work to make the disappear complete. And he needed to start to work on his story. If someone was trying to set him up, he wouldn't have much time before the cops would be knocking on the door. The body needed to be moved right away. No wonder he had a nightmare; this was a freaking mess on more than one level.

He took a deep breath and sat down for a minute, not anxious to start the work. He took the phone back out of his pocket and looked at the picture of the young, bi-racial woman, studying her face in case he had to ditch the phone quickly.

***

2:10 a.m.

"Where are you, Annie?" Rachel McCormack said to her empty living room as she pressed the menu button on her phone, closing the picture of her sister.

She turned and tossed her phone onto the black leather love seat behind her and picked the stereo remote up off the coffee table. She couldn't help looking at the framed picture of herself and her sister Antoinette hanging over the small hutch near the door to her north side condo. Their trip to California. What would Rachel's boyfriend Tim would say about her restlessness?

Tim was gone for one of his weekends, his cabin an hour from any cell tower, intentionally separated from the rest of the world. It was not often, but sometimes, especially when she and Annie hadn't spoken for a while, Rachel got a little lonely. Rachel hesitated to admit it to herself, but the mom role she adopted with Annie brought worry with it. It had been three days and no word from Annie. Their last words had been about Annie not going alone to the big party being thrown by some of the modeling and high end fashion players. Normally, she appreciated Tim's regimented, predictable life and style. Right now, though, she wanted to be able to talk to him.

"What are you up to right now, my little Annie?" Rachel asked aloud and pressed the play button on the remote.

20

She turned back around, put her hands on the keyboard of the baby grand, and closed her eyes for a moment, trying to let the blues seep into her. Her fingers strolled across the keyboard. The movement was broken, uneasy. Another glass of wine might bring the right looseness. She got up from the black piano bench and walked over to the green granite countertop in the pass-through and poured herself another glass of wine.

Despite the fact Tim insisted it was all right if she had a glass of wine every once in a while around him, it still felt awkward, as if she were somehow teasing him or throwing temptation in his face. Drinking was not often a solution to anything, but at two o'clock in the morning, when she was feeling a bit blue, a glass of wine helped bring sleep more quickly around.

As Koko Taylor's raucous, live-at-Blue's-Fest voice belted out for someone to bring her some water, Rachel walked back to the bench, took a gulp, and set the glass back on the coaster. Her body swayed with the music, and her hands started slowly, fingers finding their place and rhythm. Soon, they danced quickly across the keys, pounding heavily at times as the song reflected the anger or similar emotions that accompanied movements of the soul. She ended the song with a pounding crescendo and drank the rest of the glass.

"A cigarette and then sleep," she told herself and closed the cover over the keys.

She stood up, grabbed the lighter and pack of cigarettes off the coffee table, and walked over to the sliding glass door. As she opened the door and stepped out onto the balcony, her peripheral vision caught the picture of Tim and her at The Blue Note down on Beale Street from two years ago. It had been their first weekend together. The band, The

Memphis Blues Masters, had allowed her to come up and play piano as they covered Memphis Slim's "Steppin 'Out." That was when she knew Tim would be more than a fun fling. Although he wasn't out there on the dance floor or really seeming to get into it the way other people were, she could see he was feeling the music, and he was definitely in full support of her being herself.

She lit the cigarette and remembered when they had gone back to the hotel, and Tim had really let her in, really opened up to her. In the six months prior, she had wondered how much of his almost obsessive-compulsive behavior stemmed from being a recovering alcoholic. They had met at an AL Anon meeting, and from seeing her father overcome his habit as he got older and sicker, she knew it was often a side effect.

She looked out on the Chicago skyline. The building didn't offer a complete view, but even the rough outline was a nice horizon. Church was not going to be happening, but maybe it would be good to sleep in a bit and then go down to the House of Blues for gospel music later in the morning. The baby grand piano in her living room was a promise she had made to herself in high school after she started to get the idea that modeling might be able to take her to a place where she could afford things her parents couldn't. Her parents had been able to afford lessons for Annie and herself mostly because it was through the Baptist church they attended growing up. Although Rachel didn't belong to any one church, she still felt the connection with her music as much as she felt the connection to the blues.

Though Annie couldn't understand it, one of the aspects that she and Tim enjoyed about their relationship was that they were both independent; neither of them held back from activities simply because the other couldn't be there. They both found something more in an experience shared with someone, especially someone special, but life was not to be denied or abstained from for lack of a partner able to be there. More than once when she had gone down to the House of Blues, she had taken the opportunity to get up and play. Even if it didn't bother Tim or whomever she came with, it sometimes felt a little strange to get up and leave the people you came to breakfast with. When she went by herself, she could feel free to do whatever, and sometimes being able to play or just listen actually seemed to bring a kind of peaceful contentment to even that sense of someone missed.

"All right, Annie," Rachel said and turned to walk back in, "You and me, breakfast at Lou Mitchell's on Monday."

Rachel pulled the drapes over the sliding glass door and walked over to the kitchen. She put her glass in the dishwasher, capped the bottle, and walked it over to the refrigerator. As she opened the refrigerator door, she looked at the picture of her and Annie on their front porch, both of them smiling as they sat on their father's lap. It had been a warm summer day, their auntie was over, and daddy had been making his Daffy Duck laugh. It had been one of his favorite ways to cheer them up if there was a sad or hurt moment— scraped knees, bruised elbows and egos, and of course, the bittersweet remembrance of mama.

She closed the door and started walking toward her bedroom. That strong sense of family was one of the things that she found attractive about Tim. Although he had no siblings, he often spoke of his father, and a sort of melancholy took over when he spoke of his mother. Like her, Tim had lost his mother when he was young. Losing a parent before your fifth birthday was hard, and being able to share that with someone who really understood was something to be grateful for. Losing your mother was hard. She was the person who, even if she might not be as fun or funny as dad all the time, always brought a kind of gentle warmth to most of life and did so especially when the pain was inside. Growing up bi-racial in the seventies in that neighborhood, she and Annie had their tough days of being harshly teased.

"Take good care of them, Lord," Rachel said, thinking of her parents, together in whatever place the afterlife was. She stepped into the bathroom. As the toothpaste slid out on the brush, she knew she would sleep well—she had much to be grateful for and had been able to do well and stay on a path that would make both of her parents proud. Tomorrow would be good, and hopefully she'd talk to both Tim and Annie.

***

11:10 a.m.

Fred rolled off the plastic gloves and threw them into the bag with the clothing and other items to be burned. Having two fire pits in his spacious backyard was convenient. He would wait until he was sure no neighbors were out and then make sure the fire was very hot. There would be no mistaking it was not wood that was burning, but if he tossed it in when the fire was well-stoked, it would burn through quickly. He walked over to the sink, washed his hands, and then let the water run for at least twenty minutes, wanting to make sure everything had made its way out into the city pipes.

There had been no knock at the door, so it was not likely anyone had tipped off the police. That made it all a little weirder. *When it doesn't seem to make sense, or have a*

24

reason, that's when I worry, Fred, Sam Carlini had said. He went on to explain that predictable patterns and the kind of linear thinking that guided most people worked to their benefit. It made it easy to find an accident for them along their daily routine. Greed and revenge, the normal motivators for certain behavior, also helped to point to a direction if you were coming at it from the other end.

If this dead woman wasn't his work, and he felt that was more likely, someone had dumped the body there. Someone who thought they knew his signature style. He would have shot a target only if he was trying to send a message, and he was not a violent drunk. Someone didn't just randomly pick his house to dump the body at, especially not making it into the bedroom. He must have been really hammered for someone to get into the house and up to the bedroom. *Definitely call Tim before getting sleep*, he thought.

"Better do it now," he said aloud, starting to feel the sluggishness of exhaustion settle into his shoulders as he stretched. He reached into his pocket for his phone. "Shit, it's in the bedroom."

Fred walked slowly up the stairs to his bedroom. Tim was his sponsor, and Fred was glad to have one who seemed okay without pushing too many questions. Tim seemed okay most of the time to accept the half-explanations offered. He was an attorney though, so it was just as likely he listened well but didn't really care. Either way, he had definitely helped over the last six months. Some of it was just the willingness to listen, which was balanced by the kind of organized, disciplined manner Tim carried, kind of setting an example. And he made reference to being grateful in thought and prayer every day. Fred liked that. He took Tim's business card out of his wallet and dialed the cell number listed.

"Hey, Tim. A lawyer who answers his phone on Sunday...Sorry, sorry, just joking...Yeah, Tim. Had a backslide, pretty bad. Can we meet? Tomorrow morning...Sure. Okay, 8:30...Yeah, yeah, I'll meet you there. Thanks Tim."

That was done. Now, he was tired and knew himself well enough to know that trying to plan the next steps would not be very productive when he was this tired. A long hot shower, and then sleep. It was not just his body and mind that needed rest. He was exhausted on all levels and knew some of the processing his conscious mind needed to do might come better during and after sleep. He put the phone on the nightstand and stripped down to his underwear. He thought for a moment and then decided not to set any alarm. Better to let the body and mind take what they needed.

***

1:20 p.m.

"C'mon Annie, pick up," Rachel said, walking across the kitchen and opening the refrigerator door. She scanned the contents of the shelves. Annie's voicemail came on, and Rachel hung up. "Damn it," she mumbled. "And somehow nothing is different in the fridge from five minutes ago."

She tried to laugh at herself, but it came out odd. She wanted to deny she was worried. She knew there was nothing reasonable in her concern. There had been times when they hadn't spoken for up to a month; this had only been a week. Something about not hearing from her at all though was bothering her. Not even a gloating text about how much fun she was having. No response to any of her texts or messages since Thursday.

When they were at odds, it was not unusual for Annie to try to gloat. They hadn't really been mad at each other

26

about the party, but Rachel knew sometimes Annie felt as if she needed to push back, to do the exact opposite of advice. Rachel had decided years ago not to bring children into this crazy world, but sometimes when things were difficult between her and Annie, she felt she had an idea what it was like to be a parent. Not as much as she used to, but it still flared at times.

"Okay Rae, calm down. Call Tim and see what dinner's going to be. He'll be around tonight to talk to."

She talked to Tim at his office. He expected to be catching up on work until at least eight. He probably heard the concern in her voice, though, because he insisted she pick up something from RoSal's and come to his office around seven. He would get as much done as he could by then and organize the rest to complete on Monday. Tim had introduced her to the restaurant, and initially she had been skeptical. How many Italian restaurants on Taylor street could claim to be really better? Despite the claim by other, more well-known Italian restaurants, RoSal's was definitely the best Italian food on Taylor Street. You would probably have to go to Italy to get better. Tim knew her well. Fried ravioli and chicken RoSal's made it hard to be anything but content.

"Now," she said, taking a cigarette out of the pack on the kitchen table. "For a run." She sighed and walked toward the balcony. There were times when the insistence of people who cared about her, like Tim, made her feel a little guilty about smoking. But she smoked five cigarettes a day, maybe. On good days, less. No matter how bad a day, though, she hadn't smoked more than that since her father died.

The trip to Memphis, where she had run the marathon in just a little over four hours, was her joking argument if Tim expressed his concern about her smoking. He did run with her every once in a while, but his knees did not allow him distance. They had run one 5k together, and his time wasn't bad for a first-timer. *When you're ready to join me for the marathon in Memphis*, she would say, *then I'll consider quitting.*

She closed the balcony door and lit the cigarette. Except for the first and last of the day, she didn't have a certain time she would smoke. She knew herself, and if she just left it until her body or mind wanted it, it was easy to stay with the five. It was more often her mind that craved a cigarette from opposite ends of the mental/emotional spectrum. Stress or anxiety would call up the urge but so could the contentment of a cup of coffee or a dessert liqueur. There had been fewer occasions where she was sipping a liqueur since she started seeing Tim, but he didn't really ask her not to, so she didn't mind it. Right now, the cigarette would help reduce her stress, and the run would hopefully knock it back another notch. Whatever science had to say about the improbability of the two working together, it worked for her.

She took a deep inhale and let the smoke slowly out. Worrying was not going to make Annie respond any quicker. And if she had hooked up with somebody at the party, Rachel was fairly certain she'd be getting a selfie of the two of them on a boat somewhere, or some similar response, relatively soon. Time to run, she thought and crushed the cigarette out in the ceramic ashtray on the small table on the balcony.

***

8:20 p.m.

"Tim," Rachel said, grabbing the cigarettes from Tim and standing up. "Don't get confused. I'm not asking for your permission or approval. I'm asking for your help."

"You've said it before, Rachel," Tim replied and started condensing the leftovers into one container. "She's a bit naïve and even prone to romantic urges–maybe she's asleep on the beach in Maui right now."

"Damn it, Tim, you're doing that court room thing again," Rachel snapped. "I don't need an attorney to argue with. I need a sympathetic ear and some professional help hiring someone to find her. Try to understand how I feel. Don't throw statistical averages or analytical crap at me."

Tim looked at her for a moment, watching her tap the pack of cigarettes on the desk, before responding. He knew that he loved her, more than he ever loved his ex-wife, because it didn't bother him that she was correct about how he was behaving. He was reacting like a lawyer, thinking with that mindset, instead of addressing what she needed. His ex would never have pointed out a problem in that direct and simple of a manner—she would either have started yelling or simply walked out without saying anything.

"Okay, Rachel...sorry. It's just my lawyer instincts kicking in. But, it's only been a couple of days, and there's really nothing to indicate trouble—part of the reason the cops aren't willing to pick it up yet. She's twenty-six years old, and that party was with some of the serious players in the modeling business. People there could make tempting offers to a young, single model with strong talent. She's not as strong as you are, Rachel."

"Maybe not, but that's not the point here. Stop thinking, Tim; start feeling," Rachel said, starting to take a cigarette out of the pack, reconsidering, and tossing the pack on the table. "I know all that it's-only-Sunday-yadda-yadda crap...I'm worried about my baby sister, got a weird feeling. I need a P.I. I can trust. We don't even know if she went to that party. I haven't heard anything back from her since Thursday—that makes it four days. I'm thinking about hiring a private detective. One I can trust. I wouldn't trust the ones I've met around the modeling or acting business."

"Success smells of shadiness?" Tim replied, got up, and put the leftovers in the mini-fridge behind his desk.

"Damn straight."

"A private detective," Tim said, tossing the paper plates and remaining Styrofoam boxes in the garbage and sitting back down. The success phrase was one Rachel often used. It was not without merit, but he sometimes wondered if she really understood just how many occupations it applied to. He knew that, despite the fact that even the best detective wouldn't find Antoinette before Rachel could, he needed to let Rachel do this and even help her if he could.

"And cost is not a concern, only trustworthiness," Rachel added.

Tim looked at her and then around his small office. It was in Chicago, but not downtown. The furniture was mostly dark walnut, and the decorations were tasteful but modest. Not like the office he once had on Dearborn. Rachel could afford to think like that. Despite her comment on success, she was successful and had scruples. She didn't know what it was like to thirst for...*trustworthy private detective!* he yelled silently at himself, pushing back the urge to think about the taste of a gimlet.

"Trustworthy. There was a guy I met a while back, before the...I got myself on track. Trying to think of his name...Mark...Mark Hamilton. He was one of those people who wouldn't work for clients he thought might be connected to anything criminal, or...he had a phrase...*otherwise lacking in conscientious culpability.* He was quite a character."

"Sounds good to me," Rachel replied and walked back over to the desk, stepping next to Tim and placing her hands on his shoulders, massaging firmly. "Look forward, don't dwell."

"Thank you," Tim replied, allowing her hands to relieve the tenseness. She was not the human being he had confessed the exact nature of his wrongs to, but she knew he was recovering and seemed to accept the man she knew him to be. Antoinette had always had suspicions.

"You think he's still honest?"

"Still honest? I wouldn't doubt it. He had that standard that kept him working too hard for someone as smart as he was. The question is whether or not he's still in business."

"Well," Rachel said, leaning over Tim and turning on his desktop computer. "There's only one way to find out."

A simple Google search and a phone call told them Mark Hamilton was indeed still in the private investigations business and was willing to meet them the next day at ten o'clock. Tim was not particularly enthused by the prospect but knew that it would make Rachel happy if she felt she were doing something. Fortunately, Rachel knew he had two major contract negotiations ready to wind up, so he would be mostly on the periphery lending moral support, and it would be okay. Better to offer what help he could than to be asked.

"I'll see if any of my clients I know from the music and entertainment industries might know something about the party. It's a long shot, but maybe somebody they know would be able to ask around to find out if she was there."

"That, Tim," Rachel said and wrapped her arms around him, "is one of the reasons I think you're a keeper. Even though you're not exactly warm and fuzzy on the surface, you've got warm and fuzzy hiding inside."

Tim hugged her back. Neither of them would necessarily have been described as warm and fuzzy, although Rachel was a bit more social. When they had first met at Al-Anon, the physical attraction, that underlying basis for at least the start of most human romance, was immediate. It was also the combination of simple candor about difficult matters and witty, sometimes self-deprecating, remarks in conversation that seemed to be what she appreciated. Their first three dates had been over breakfast. They both agreed breakfast was the best meal to get out regularly. Warm and fuzzy though, he thought, was probably not exactly the right phrase. Now, though, was not the time for correcting.

"So, are you saying I'm within the size limit?"

"You do pretty well," Rachel said, a grin growing at the corners of her mouth. One hand moved down, rubbing his glutes. "Especially for a white guy."

"That kind of profiling, young lady, might earn you a spanking."

"Promises, promises," Rachel said and pulled him closer. He squeezed her tightly and then slapped her tight, toned posterior. She responded by pressing into him, and he knew the flesh was taking control. For very different reasons, it was something they both needed. Physical intimacy had not been difficult for them, and even though sometimes he worried it was too important an aspect of their relationship, once started, the dance wanted completion. His hand moved to the base of her neck, fingers reaching into and pulling back her hair. His head moved down and forward, his lips and teeth finding the flesh of her neck, and they were both lost to it.

CHAPTER TWO

Monday, June 17th
8:30 a.m.

Sitting in the booth of the small diner, Fred flipped the business card over and over with the thumb and two fingers of his right hand. He stopped to look at it for a moment. *Timothy E. Vanderschmidt, attorney at law. Specializing in entertainment and copyright law.* That's my sponsor, Fred thought.

He couldn't help but think about the first time he realized he had a problem, well before he had a sponsor. It had been a little over a year ago. No one wound up dead over it, but it shook him up pretty good. Losing track of even a couple of hours when you were responsible for protecting the Justino family, and not getting caught, was too dangerous.

That day, he had been walking from the Rosemont Holiday Inn. Back then, the Allstate Arena was still called the Rosemont Horizon. And—he smiled as he sat back for a moment—Mayor Stephens had still been dancing around the questions about his connections to Chicago's Italian mob bosses. Indictments aside, he was considered one of the best front men. That had been when he spotted Tommy Johnson, standing by the edge of the parking lot, having a smoke. Despite the fact that he worked security for the hotel, Fred thought Tommy was someone he could talk to. Tommy got his job based mostly on his military experience, not from being a suburban cop. Tommy was the kind of guy who understood how the world worked. He knew enough about what went on in Rosemont, River Forest, Melrose, and other places to know what to report or not. People of color, they seemed to be more like real people.

"Tommy," Fred said, taking a step toward the short, stocky black man. "I need to talk to you. You okay to talk?"

"I always got time for you, Mr. Batiste," Tommy replied and dropped the cigarette butt. "There's two other officers on duty, and nothing happening."

"Look," Fred said and took his wallet out of his pants pocket. He flipped it open quickly and deftly took out a hundred dollar bill. He palmed the bill and put the wallet back. "This has got to stay between me 'n you, know what I mean?"

Fred reached over, shaking hands with Tommy.

"I understand, sir. But this ain't hardly necessary. I like you, Mr. Batiste. You're one of the quietest, most respectful people I know who eats here regular. Truth is, least half the people I see here regular wouldn't even talk to someone like me."

"Just Fred. Call me Fred. Tommy, I got trouble...that is, a problem. I, well...shit...I think I might be losin' a little control over part of my life. And, well..."

"Go ahead, Fred," Tommy said, cocking his head to the side a little. "I see those eyes looking around. Trust me, there's no one around that's going to be paying any attention—I'm just doing my rounds, and unless a call comes up, nobody's going to be looking for me for at least another twenty minutes."

"Tommy," Fred said, rubbing his hands together, wishing he had a drink. "I don't want this to sound, you know, prejudiced or anything. It's just, well, I figure you might be able to help me more with this kinda problem than most people I know."

"Like what, Fred? I know you've probably seen some trouble, runnin' with that crowd of Italian businessmen."

"Yeah, I've seen a few things. Not all those businessmen are exactly lily white. But I never had times...trouble like times where I can't remember things or always feel like I got to have a drink."

"Fred, relax. You're going to rub all the skin off those hands."

"Tommy, I can't relax. I think...I think I got a serious drinking problem, and I don't know what to do about it. Like, the other day, I lost a couple hours completely. There, that's it, I said it."

"Damn, Fred," Tommy replied, a slight grin appearing at the corners of his mouth. "I'm sorry; I guess I shouldn't act like it's funny. I know it's not funny. You just had me worried man, acting like you killed someone or something like that. My brother went through a hard time with drinking. Well that, and some other shit he was taking. First thing you do, get yourself down to a meeting, get yourself into a twelve step."

"Twelve step? I didn't say I got a dancing problem, Tommy."

"Probably you do, though," Tommy replied. A grin flashed quickly across his face and disappeared even quicker. "Sorry. Look, twelve steps is a kind of program. It's more than just people telling you what you already know. It's...well, it works."

"Yeah, but I wouldn't want everyone..."

"Fred, nobody going to know unless you tell them. It's one of the things about twelve steps: except for what you do with your sponsor, everything stays at the meetings. You think it's a bunch of shame, and they know that, even if it isn't. You'd be surprised how many people you know have gone through it, and probably there's a lot more need to. Just call up and find a meeting. Hell, pick somewhere away from work and home. AA is pretty much everywhere these days, and it's other ones out there too."

"Twelve steps, huh? And it works? You're straight with me?"

"As an arrow, Fred. Sorry about the bad humor. Twelve steps—you and God, Creator, Yahweh...whatever you call your higher power, Fred. It's all you need if you got that kind of trouble."

"All right, all right," Fred replied and stepped over to his car. "Twelve steps it is. I'll see you later, Tommy. And thanks, Tommy."

"More coffee, sir?" the waitress asked.

Fred jerked and then sat back quickly. "What? Oh, yes, please...Miranda," Fred replied, brushing aside the momentary surprise of being taken out of the memory and reading the name tag on the girl's blouse. "You're new, huh?"

"Yes, sir. In from Cali."

"California. That's a big change. You didn't like it out there?"

"I did. A little too much. Easy to get caught up in it. Like the song, you know?"

"The song? Oh, you mean the Eagles. Yeah. Yeah, I get it," Fred answered, a bit surprised himself that he understood what she meant.

"Fred, you hitting on young waitresses again?" Tim asked as he walked over to the other side of the table. "Although, you have good taste."

"Coffee, sir?"

"Yes, please, Miranda. And another menu."

Fred smiled at Miranda and waited until she had started to walk away before he began talking to Tim. Looking at Tim, impeccably attired this early on a Monday morning, always wearing his dress coat, no matter the weather, Fred couldn't help but wonder if perhaps Tim's problem had not been quite so bad. Fred hesitated for a moment. Although he heard other people talking openly about their problems, he was still not comfortable with the idea. He wasn't quite sure yet whether it was because of the nature of his job to speak little or being embarrassed.

"Thanks for coming, Tim. I...I figured you were the best person to talk to."

"That's what a sponsor is here for. Luckily, Mondays are one of my office days. I have a ten o'clock appointment I have to be at, though."

"Do you like that? I mean, being in front of a judge and all those people?"

"Hmm. Is that a legitimate question or avoiding the subject?"

"Do all sponsors cut straight to the chase like that? Don't get me wrong, it's good. I like that."

"As a general rule, a good sponsor tries to cut through the bullshit—it helps people to stop trying to fool themselves. Sort of, you know, forces you to look at it, instead of away."

"Makes sense. That's good. Sort of like that scene in..."

"Fred," Tim interjected calmly but forcefully. "Why did you call me? What happened?"

"Jesus, Tim, I don't know what happened. That's the fu...freakin' problem: I don't know what happened. For like a good four or more hours, completely blank."

"All right, slow down," Tim said, putting a hand on Fred's arm and looking over to Miranda as she walked up to the table. "I'll have the Southwestern omelet, fruit on the side, and the hash browns, crispy—and yes, I know that's extra. Fred?"

"Wha? Oh, yeah. I'll have the…gypsy skillet."

"How did you want your eggs, sir?"

"Fred, just call me Fred. Over medium, rye toast."

Miranda scribbled down their order and walked away.

Fred explained to Tim that he had absent-mindedly had the first drink at a small party on Saturday, wasn't sure how many he had after that, and thought it was around eight or nine that he completely blacked out.

"You made it home without hurting yourself, anyone else, or destroying your car?"

"I…yes."

"Fred, I can tell you're still not sure about that. And that's what you need to think about: not even knowing whether or not you've harmed someone. Get to a meeting. Have you told any of your family about your recovery yet?"

"Not yet. It's hard…the…my fu…family, I don't know that they'd understand."

"You'll have to talk to them eventually, Fred. Sooner rather than later; it'll make it easier."

"Right," Fred replied and moved his hands from the table as he saw Miranda approaching with the food. Tim always kept conversations short and to the point. He was all about the program and keeping everything on track and in order. Fred imagined Tim's office and home were neat and clean. It was good.

Tim never seemed to question his stories, and after he attended his first few meetings, Fred knew he needed a sponsor he could lie to. Tim didn't seem to notice when he had almost slipped and said *the family*. Tim didn't seem to miss much, but he was human too.

"Thank you," Tim said to Miranda as she put their plates in front of them.

"Anything else, gentleman?"

"More coffee, please," Fred replied.

"Right away, sir."

"Fred, just Fred, Miranda."

"I'm doing pretty good with my swearing though, not bringing the Lord's name into it. When I was younger, I could never make sense of that, but when you explained it at that meeting, how we assign value and insult God when we do that, I got it."

"A little progress is better than none, Fred. Have you talked to your employer about a new position?"

"Not yet. That's kind of a big step, Tim. Do you go to court much with that entertainment stuff?" Fred asked, knowing they had said everything that really needed to be said. Neither he nor Tim were really small talk kind of people, but learning about someone's job or a different kind of life was always interesting. As he tasted the first mouthful of his skillet waiting for Tim's response, Fred felt maybe this could all fade away as long as he could get himself on track like Tim.

***

9:50 a.m.

"Why all the way out in Elgin?" Rachel asked, setting her chai latte back in the cup holder.

"Fits Mark," Tim replied and flipped on the turn signal as they approached the Route 31 off ramp. "He frequently

40

referred to Crook County as no place for an honest detective or lawyer."

"Crook County," Rachel echoed, watching as they drove past the sign for the Grand Victoria Casino. "Hmm…and there's a boat down in Aurora, too; doesn't seem like Kane County is immune from influence."

"I don't think Mark would argue that. Better not to get him started on the subject. As I remember, he does like to talk at length when a subject interests him."

"Tim," Rachel said, slapping him lightly on the shoulder.

There were times when Rachel wondered about that very practical, almost cold side of Tim. He was always polite, but he wasn't always friendly. He had confessed to her about his being a recovering alcoholic right away after they had met at a release party for one of the new names at Carrot Top, but other than his first's wife narcissistic neurosis, he hadn't really shared much about other factors that started him down the road.

Who, after all, didn't like to talk at length about subjects that interested them? Was that sometimes-cynical side of Tim a purely circumstantial cynicism? Most of the cynical people she knew, whether they realized it or would admit it, were cynics born of life circumstances, as opposed to the flat, dull, fatalistic view of a true cynic. A true cynic was devoid of anger or bitterness. Tim did seem to have some of the anger, and his recovering alcoholic status probably explained that. She didn't know all that had driven him to drinking but accepted that she might not ever know either. Some of it had to be left behind sometimes. Scars too easily became reopened wounds.

"What was the name of the restaurant again? Paul's?"

"You didn't write it down, Tim? You?"

"Very funny, Rachel. I did write it down, but the notepad is on the back seat, and it wouldn't surprise me if that Elgin officer would pull us over if I were reaching back there."

"Navigator will tell you where to turn," Rachel replied, looking at the black and white police car backed into a spot in the parking lot for the Restore and other businesses. "Elgin's not exactly Glencoe or anything."

"No, but I'm pretty sure they have more officers than crime during most early afternoons. And, revenue is revenue."

"Yeah, but you're white and driving a Lexus SUV. You really think they'd pull you over for anything other than speeding, maybe?"

"Hmm, unfortunately, you have a good point. Should we let you drive on the way out then?"

"Maybe another day. Not in the theory-testing mood at the moment, funny guy."

She looked out the window at nothing in particular and felt his hand reach over and squeeze her knee. It was only Tuesday, but without hearing from Annie at all, it seemed a long time since Friday. She knew the different paths the modeling industry could take, and some of them didn't end well. Addiction, mental illness, two or three failed marriages, or worse. Most people got out before it got too bad, but the lure of fame was strong.

"Always remember, my Rae-Rae," her father had said, sitting on the porch, a Manhattan in one hand, a Kool in the other. He pointed a finger from the hand holding the drink at her. "Don't let the world, don't let nobody tell you you need a man to be okay."

She had been eleven on that sweltering August day. Dog days they called them. Days when you opened the neighborhood fire hydrant or, if you could afford it, took public transportation to the beach. Nights you slept in the basement, unless you were still small enough to sneak into your parents bed, where the window unit was. Central air was not very common in the brownstones and brick bungalows that made up much of the south side neighborhood, but most folks had at least one or two window units in the house. She had just completed her first modeling assignment for David and Lee, a clothing catalogue shoot, and it was the first anniversary of her mother's death.

"Why? What you mean, daddy?"

"Your mama, she didn't *need* me here. Coulda done it without me. Post office work ain't exactly what most people think of as a career. She worked hard, though, and knew to take advantage of opportunities. Driving a bus don't pay no better. But, she *wanted* me here, and I wanted to be here. So we could take care of each other and you girls."

"You miss her a lot, daddy?"

"My baby Rae-Rae, if I didn't have you and your sister, I'd be drinking a lot more of these," he said and raised the glass, a tear rolling down one cheek.

"I love you, daddy," she had said and stepped over to him, leaning in to give him a hug.

"You just remember that. You can do anything you want. Get some of that modeling money into a school savings. And if the Lord calls me to be with your mother before that child is grown, keep an eye on Antoinette. I think your mother and I may have been a little too easy. She came as kind of a late surprise, and we maybe let ourselves think with the ten years between you, she'd have someone she could look up to

43

for examples. She always was a little more shy than you, maybe a little more afraid of the world. But, seems more often now that she takes a liking to getting attention. Remember that for you, and for her."

"I'll remember, daddy. I promise."

"Okay, Rae. Now, you run down to your Auntie's and get that girl. Time you get back, I'll have this drink finished, and we'll get over to church."

He had stood up and wrapped her in a hug.

"Rachel," Tim said, his hand gently squeezing her knee, bringing her back to the moment. "We're here."

***

"Unfortunately," Mark said, taking a sip from what she thought must be at least his ninth cup of coffee. "Tim's probably right."

"What do you mean? Can't you private detectives get information about where somebody last used their credit card and stuff?"

"If you believe the fiction, there's very little we can't do."

"Mark," Tim interjected.

"Okay, right. Sorry Rachel. What people believe we can do thanks to the fiction is, well, a bit far from the reality. With certain information, law enforcement has quicker, more direct access. Sometimes they don't think to access it, or, unfortunately for us, they don't see this as a police matter yet. Hopefully, she's not in lock-up anywhere, but I'll check that possibility too. There are definitely some information sources I can try that might give us a starting point."

"Like?"

"Like, I'll run a top tier comprehensive background check. That will tell us all about her up until the last few months. May be some things you don't or don't want to know about your baby sister. Sometimes, we get lucky and there's something more recent. Worst case scenario, it'll give me everything I need to know to get started."

"Get started?" Rachel asked, not worried the concern and frustration in her voice was obvious.

"I understand how you feel," Mark said, taking his phone out of his chest pocket and rapidly pressing buttons. He held it out to her, showing her a picture of two little boys, wearing similar outfits and matching Captain America hats and holding cotton candy cones that looked almost as tall as they were. "I wouldn't like what I was hearing either if it was about those boys. But, I need to be honest. She's a model who was at a party with and for some big names in the business, right? It makes no sense for me to go chasing after her until I see who she really is. And, no offense intended, a lot of people are surprised what they didn't know about family."

"None taken. Are you really that good?" Rachel asked. She had been impressed that Mark had remembered some details about Tim. His wool dress coat worn irrespective of the weather apparently was something that went back to darker days. She was glad for that, though, because part of her felt it was the discipline, the dress and other standards, that kept Tim on track.

"You'll find out in a couple days. Fortunately, those two boys are on vacation with their mom, and I just closed two cases last week. It'll be sooner if I can make that happen. And remember what I said: don't hold the emotions back as long as they're not controlling you. Sometimes they even jar a memory that can help. Here's my card. Let me write my cell on the back."

As he wrote the number down, Rachel looked at him. Unbuttoned flannel shirt and a Veterans for Peace t-shirt worn underneath, even in the middle of summer. His long hair woven as if he were some kind of latter-day Native American. He had a pen, but it was plastic and had some kind of ad for an oil change place on it. His notebook was dog-eared and appeared to have coffee stains at the edge. She could only imagine what his office must look like. She couldn't help but wonder. She looked over at Tim. Tim nodded and closed his eyes for a second. He was satisfied. Mark certainly seemed confident. He was personable and seemed genuine. If Tim was saying to trust him that was enough for Rachel.

***

1:20 p.m.

Fred wasn't sure if Rossi was the best place to start, but he was certain Rossi would be someone who knew enough to keep their conversation to himself. Rossi understood that Fred moved with impunity, and unless Don Justino himself put something out that Fred was not to be talked to, it could be assumed you talked to Fred. If nothing else, Rossi would know if anything had been said about him and if there were any retirement plans. Rossi was good, but even Rossi would give enough away in his responses that Fred would know if he had anything to worry about.

"Good morning, sir," the short, blonde receptionist said as Fred walked into the offices of Morgan & Bernstein, P.C.

"Good morning, young lady. How are you?"

"Very well, thank you, sir. Did you have an appointment?"

"I do. Edward Rossi at 1:30. I try to be early."

"And your name, sir?"

"Just let him know Fred is here."

"Very good, sir."

Fred sat down in one of the overstuffed leather chairs, pretended to look at the selection of magazines for the bored and wealthy, and listened as the secretary called to Rossi's office. Even the smallest of details could prove to be important in matters of this nature. A slight hesitation in her voice, or something similar, might indicate what would await him in Rossi's office. She hung up and walked over to him.

"You can go back now, sir."

"Thank you."

Fred walked down the hallway and hesitated outside Rossi's office. The double glass doors were open, and Rossi stood at the far end of his office, looking out his large picture window, which gave him an excellent view of downtown Chicago. His hands were behind his back, clasped together, hanging just below his belt line. The king looking out over his kingdom. There was no question Rossi acted like that at times, and, at least with respect to the mayor and other government officials, he did have more influence than they did. But, Fred thought, a quick smile flashing across his face, Rossi needed to remember he was still responsible to others and could be replaced.

"Mr. Rossi, sir," Fred said, stepping into the office. "How are you?"

"'Mr. Rossi?' Fred," Rossi said, turned, and walked over to Fred, his arms held out wide. "We know each other better than that."

They hugged, patted each other on the back a couple times, and ended with a strong hand shake, Fred holding Rossi's hand between his two. They looked at each other and smiled. Rossi motioned for Fred to take a seat on the leather couch opposite his desk. Fred looked at the couch and then at the chairs adjacent each end of it. Wanting his back to a wall, Fred sat down in the center of the couch.

"So, Fred, is this strictly business or do you have some time to tell me how you've been?"

"I've been good, but unfortunately I do have to keep this short. I hope you understand. It's not personal; we can maybe catch up another day. I do want to know how your little girl is doing at the Geoffrey."

"I understand. Do you need a legal favor or some information?"

"Just some information, if you have any."

"Hopefully, I can help. Can I get you a drink?"

"No, no thanks. You can go ahead if you want though."

"No," Rossi replied and walked over to Fred, his eyes darting from Fred to his desk.

"I haven't had an assignment in a while, but I heard some talk that we might be moving some more people into modeling and fashion, maybe trying to influence some of the younger talent to sign with our companies."

"Well, I think that's always true to some degree, Fred. What did you hear that brings you to me?"

"Nothing specific really," Fred lied, glad he had asked that question first. Rossi gave away that there was something specific to be heard. "I guess there's some talk out there about one or two young models that could bring a lot of money?"

"Talk is cheap, Fred, you know that. I know nothing about anyone looking for a specific person to bring into the family."

48

"Hmm, that's good to know. I was just thinking, sometimes when that kind of thing is happening, it sometimes means I need to assist with problem personnel who might try to dissuade people from taking a good offer."

"That's a good thing about you, Fred, you're always thinking. No, as I said, I haven't heard anything like that. Was that all?"

"That was all, Ed. Thank you for seeing me on short notice."

"The pleasure is always mine, Fred."

Fred stood up and stepped over to him. They hugged again and then walked over to the office doors. Rossi offered his hand, and they shook again, this time more cordially. Fred nodded and patted Rossi on the shoulder.

"Thanks again, Ed. Hopefully, I'll see you soon and we can really talk."

"That would be good, Fred. We'll have a drink."

Fred smiled and turned. As he walked down the hallway, Fred thought about what he had learned. There was something happening about a specific model. Rossi didn't really answer his question. Most lawyers didn't know how to answer a question directly, but there was something more. He avoided telling Fred what he knew by stating what he didn't know. He was not nervous or anxious, though, and talked about having a drink in the future. People like Rossi, people with a little too much faith in themselves, typically gave themselves away by what they didn't say. Had he not mentioned getting together soon, Fred would have known he didn't expect to see Fred again. Fortunately, Fred thought, Rossi's comment about thinking was a reflection of his belief Fred was not a thinking man. Like many people in the family, Rossi assumed Fred was a cardboard cut-out of an old world hit man who thought only about completing assignments and making money. *Now*, Fred thought, *I have to find out if there was a connection between the girl, the party and his standing in the family.*

CHAPTER THREE

Tuesday, June 21st
5:45 a.m.

Fred got out of bed quickly. Although no one had ever accused him of being *chipper*, he was definitely a morning person.   Looking in the mirror as he squeezed some toothpaste out, he thought, chipper was like spunky; he never had much appreciation for spunky. He began brushing, going over his mental checklist for the day. He had found a meeting the night before in Frankfort. The far south suburb was like many of the northern and western suburbs. The influence of the family was so well covered by legitimate fronts, people there romantically imagined they were far from the kind of corruption found in Chicago. And, having a story why you happened to be at a different place for a meeting was easy. People at AA meetings were frequently in and out of different locations.

He had managed to liquefy most of the body and cut up the bones into tiny pieces. Even now, that kind of thought bothered him.   Clean up work was very different than anything else. It was a little creepy, weird. And, knowing this had not been an assignment, Fred couldn't help feeling a little worse. She had been an attractive woman. Had they met at the party? There had been no calls or visits from police yet. If someone was trying to set him up, they would have shown up in twenty-four to forty-eight.   It was the only possibility making sense at the moment though. If he had done this, even in a drunken state, he would not have removed all her identification and papers from her small clutch. He would have left everything inside and burned or otherwise gotten rid of everything at once. Someone had cleaned everything out, but not thoroughly enough. In a small inside corner pocket of her St. Laurent jumper jacket was a business card. *Rachel McCormack, Fashion Photographer.* If he couldn't get somewhere on his own, he would have Bert Ratso get information about the photographer. Fred didn't like to use Ratso unless he had no other choice. Ratso was good because he was the kind of private detective who knew the value of money and not much else. He didn't ask a lot of questions and gave you a lot of information quickly without any disclaimers or other nonsense. That also meant he was subject to the influence of other people's money and the intimidation of authority figures who could convince him he was about to lose a lot of it. Sometimes he was the only available option. Fred was going to try to avoid taking it.

"Time to talk to a couple people," Fred said to the face in the mirror. He knew he was close to retirement, but this would not be how that was typically handled. Too risky. A specialist had to be retired permanently in most instances. If they could be trusted, they were moved far away and settled into a very quiet lifestyle. Fred thought his work for the family had brought him respect and gratitude, but Don Justino was talking of retiring as well. That could mean some changes in how things were typically handled. "After a good work out."

***

Twelve miles, one hundred push-ups, and twenty minutes worth of planks later, Fred was getting out of the shower, feeling better than he had in four days. Focused. He had to go try to talk to the people he knew who had been at the party. Anyone who knew him would be sure to remark about his leaving with the woman. He thought Michael DiNino had been there, but he had left early. Sal and Tommy, who kept an eye and hand on providing entertainment, especially for the modeling and movie business for the family, would know about the party. It was not surprising that even a party that was not organized by the family was still overseen by it. Their offices first.

***

"Look, Fred, it's like Sal said," Tommy Connelly explained and stepped from behind the desk. "The party was not family business. Michael came to us unexpected the next day, asking about some model. My people told me she was at the party but not a lot more. One of the bouncers thinks he saw her leave with some shyster in the business."

Fred looked at them. Tommy Connelly, his ruddy complexion and telling orange hair trimmed short, and his partner Sal Gianconno, black hair and olive complexion, looked like a poster for some campaign about people learning to work together. No matter whose story you wanted to believe, the Irish perspective or the Italian one, hard lessons had been learned from the Tammany Hall days. It was another thing he and Sam Carlini had talked about: history. How important it was to remember the stories people tell themselves. *From the Jews and the Muslims to the Americans and the Indians, people's convenient memory often informed their history more than anything else,* Sam had said. Sometimes, if you wanted to stay alive, it was best to honor whatever version of the truth was the accepted standard. Don Justino and those in his close confidence were not always right, but telling them that was not always an advisable course of action.

"Two more questions," Fred said. He sat up straight, leaned over, and slowly placed his elbows on Sal's desk, bringing his palms together, fingers intertwining and folding, his chin coming to rest on his thumbs, his eyes locking with Sal's. "Did he get a good look at the shyster? Did anyone say they saw other people from the family there?"

Fred knew that Sal was smart enough to recognize the posture as both intimidating and simply asking for the truth. Sal's eyes held his. Sal did not blink, nor did he look away before answering the question.

"He said he was a white guy he's seen around before, and someone told him he was an attorney, but he doesn't know that for sure. Doesn't know his name. Very average looking, salt and pepper hair, early fifties."

"Hmmmm," Fred replied without making any movement or motion. He closed his eyes for a second and then opened them to continue his direct stare. "And..."

"One of the managers, someone who knows nothing, described someone who looked like you being there. Didn't know who you—this guy—was and only noticed you because you came alone, were slamming shots with a group of people, then left alone. Thought it was odd you hadn't hooked up with someone."

"You got some good managers, Sal," Fred replied and sat back, satisfied. "Did you have cameras rolling?"

"No, not at these parties. What is it, Fred? What's going on with this girl?"

"Tommy, Tommy, my little Irish friend. You know better than that. If you were supposed to know, you already would."

Fred knew the lie would satisfy them because overall it was the truth. Right now, he wanted more than anything else to know what was going on. But he knew more than when he arrived. The girl had left with some shyster. Whether he was an entertainment attorney, just a friend of someone, or maybe even someone trying to network business, that was what Fred knew he had to find out. He stood up and walked to the office door.

"Gentlemen," Fred said and put his hand on the doorknob. "I trust you'll have the good sense to forget this conversation ever took place."

"Sal," Tommy said, smiling and turning to his partner. "You know, I wonder what ever happened to Fred. I don't think I've seen him since the wedding last year."

Fred smiled and nodded. He opened the door and walked out of their offices. At least there was some information to work with, a starting point to go from. Maybe Edward Rossi could add a little more to the picture. He was one of the few attorneys in the inner circle and so might know something about the attorney at the party. And Detective Antonio Vincenzo was last on the list. Fred didn't like to think about calling in markers, but Antonio and Edward both owed him a favor. If those three points of contact couldn't give him enough information, Bert Ratso would be the last shot before taking it directly to Don Justino. He knew Michael DiNino's involvement meant he would be able to talk to Don Justino if he couldn't get any answers on his own. Michael was a straight shooter, or he wouldn't be close to Don Justino. He had not met Michael and was not really curious at this point—he was sure he didn't want anyone else being able to put a face with his name right now.

As he pushed the elevator call button, he looked back at the glass double doors that opened into the offices of Connelly and Gianconno. *Entertainment Consultants*, Fred thought. Now that was a funny twist on the kind of consulting that really comprised the majority of money made at their business, even if it didn't represent the day to day. As the elevator opened and Fred stepped in, finding a place within the huddled group of people but with his back against the wall, he smiled. If these people only knew, he thought.

***

6:45 a.m.

As Fred had been closing in on mile six, Tim watched as a red-tailed hawk floated across the sky; a slight tip of its wings and the circle became a sharp, diving arc. The hawk appeared to be picking up speed as it descended, and Tim pulled out a cigarette, holding up the inscribed silver Zippo but not lighting it. A few feet from what appeared to be a crash landing, the hawk's wings suddenly flapped furiously, and its talons found their target, a garter snake that had slithered out onto the shoulder of the road to sun itself. As the hawk immediately began a return to the air, Tim smiled and lit his cigarette. *Nature had a way*, he thought.

He inhaled deeply, closing his eyes for a moment. This area of the forest preserve was not where he normally went for a break before the onslaught of the day, but something in him wanted a change, a change to someplace where he was less likely to see anyone he knew. This part of the forest preserve, somewhere between Park Ridge and Des Plaines, on the edge of Chicago but not in the city, seemed appropriate. He knew it had a reputation for attracting some of the seedier element, as well as for being a haven for gay men who were involved in affairs of one sort or another. People were interesting, Tim thought. They had a penchant for associating anything different with the dirty or dark side.

"Good morning," someone said, the voice a light, lilting baritone.

Tim turned to see the short, casually dressed young man approaching him from the path that led into the woods. By the tone of his voice, the ease of his walk, and the fact his hands were in his pockets, Tim knew that this young man was not someone he need fear. The New Balance running shoes, newer-looking short-sleeved shirt, and worn-but-clean jeans told Tim this was not someone who was living on the edge. *At least, not financially*, he thought.

"Yes, it is. Good morning to you, young man."

"Look, I know you don't know me from Adam and all that, but I forgot my cigarettes in my…"

"Say no more," Tim interjected and reached into his jacket pocket, pulling out and holding open the pack of Newports for the stranger. "Take two if you need to."

"No, thanks, but I'm good. Just one to get me back to the ranch."

"Very good then. Morning walk?"

"Yeah. Bit of peace before the day gets crazy."

"Oh, I know. Believe me, young man, I know about that stress and aggravation. People wanting more and more from you. Pace getting faster every day. Always someone with something to say."

"Yeah…sometimes it's like you want to say, 'relax, have a drink or something.'"

"Precisely. A good couple of gin and tonics. Straighten out the rough spots. Put people…things back in order."

"Rrright. Okay, well, I gotta get going. Thanks for the smoke. Have a good one."

"You're welcome. You do the same, young man."

Tim watched as the young man walked away. He wasn't sure what he had said or done, but he could tell a shift had occurred, and the stranger had felt the need to move on.

God knows, Tim thought, *even people like him could be judgmental.* People who had no real experience in life. Living in the suburbs. Never knowing the challenges of fast-paced, competitive city living or the simple, hard-working country life either. Somewhere in an in-between nether world of keeping up with the latest food processor and new age spirituality. Fooling themselves that by not choosing between the temptations of the city or the simplicity of the country they were somehow outside the realm of judgment, as if their passive church-once-a-week before the football game was buying them time.

At the gritty sound of tires rolling across the pebble-strewn forest preserve road, Tim looked over. Park police. Another revenue-generating tool of a thoroughly corrupt government. Of course, in the United States, because the corruption occurred in board rooms between men wearing suits and discussing things obtusely, and because cash never directly passed between people, the common misconception was that America was a shining example of virtuous government serving the people, keeping justice at the forefront in a Christian nation. God only knew how many real Christians there were any more in the country.

"Good morning, officer. Beautiful day," Tim said as the cruiser slowly rolled up to him.

"Mornin' sir. Little bit of peace and quiet before you join the rat race?"

"Well said," Tim replied, smiling at the overweight, middle-aged man behind the wheel. Of course he wore mirrored aviator sunglasses as if he were a state trooper and might actually have to confront a real criminal. Not that he could chase anyone down if he had to. "Nature is the best escape from it all."

"Couldn't agree with you more on that, sir. Just be careful if you go down by the pond. Had a couple of rattlesnake bites in the last few weeks. Not deadly or anything, but definitely ruin your day."

"Indeed. Thank you, officer. Just headed out to start the grind. Have a good day."

"You do the same, sir. Keep your head above it all."

"I'll do my best," Tim said, smiling and turning to walk back to his car. As if the lazy patronage worker knew what it meant to keep your head above the filthy mess of society. As he walked back to the car, Tim sorted through the people he needed to talk to. It was mostly a matter of whom to talk to first because as soon as he talked to someone, word would get out that he was asking questions. He knew Don Justino wouldn't be concerned as long as nothing went outside the family, but some of the lesser people like Edward Rossi would still try to make something of it. Rossi was so small-minded. He had to be able to look Rachel in the eye and tell her he was making an effort to see what might have happened to Antoinette. Rossi first? Or Connelly and Gianconno?

***

9:50 a.m.

"Tim was gone for the weekend, Mark," Rachel replied, walking through the office door and then back toward Mark's desk. "Once a month he does this retreat thing at a family cabin. He's been doing it for years. Helps him keep focused, he says. Goes up there, shuts his phone off, canoes, fishes, all that."

Rachel didn't want to sit down. She was restless. She looked at the diplomas, certificates, and other materials hanging on the wall behind Mark's desk. Private Detective

59

license, certified firearms instructor license, some military diplomas, and then a Veterans for Peace patch next to another that read UFPJ. She stepped over to the wall and pointed to one of the US Army Military Police certificates.

"What is SRT?"

"Special Reactions Team. Military Police version of S.W.A.T. Exotic weapons, specialized tactical training."

"And a firearm instructor license. But you're a member of Veterans for Peace?"

"Yes, ma'am. I like to think I've grown a little since I was twenty. And I got the firearms instructor license while I was working for another company. Haven't taught a class since I left that company to go out on my own—sixteen years ago."

"Don't like guns?"

"Don't like people carrying who shouldn't be—training standards are too lax. And the truth of firearms in this line of work is that they're more likely to cause problems than resolve them. I keep a couple in the office, but like the two private detectives I worked for before I got my own license, generally I don't carry."

Mark's phone rang; he looked at the caller ID read-out and held up his index finger in a wait-a-minute gesture. Rachel turned and walked to the bookcases on the other side of the room, the side that looked as much like personal space as business office. There was a row of three filing cabinets and two bookcases along the adjoining wall. One of the bookcases was full of Criminal Law and Procedure type books; the other was quite different. *The Bible According to Mark Twain*, Ray Bradbury...and she thought she had seen some cartoon books.

The middle row of that bookcase also had a set of photographs. Mark and his boys fishing, camping, and otherwise at play in the outdoors. Rachel couldn't help but notice that none of the pictures included a mom. And there was an abalone shell on a wooden stand with a small bag of some kind of herb underneath it. That possibly explained the not-unpleasant, light, musky odor. Interesting.

"Sorry about that," Mark said. "So, you were saying Tim retreats to a cabin in the north woods. Getting back to nature?"

"Tim? No. Not in the sense you mean it. He's not like a Thoreau or Emerson type. Not like a roughing-it kind of guy most of the time either. I think some of it may be sort of spiritual in a way—his parents were very religious; I think his father was a priest or reverend. But mostly I think it's a break from the business, from high pressure litigation and legal consulting."

"Yeah, he doesn't strike me as either a Greenpeace or a Bass Masters kind of guy. All right, well I should still talk to him a little more later—he's bound to know at least some people in the system who could make some checks easier. But, you're really my client. The first set of reports are back, and there are some questions."

"I thought the reports would bring answers," Rachel said.

"Doesn't really work like that. Especially because we don't even know what, if anything, has happened to her. This is essentially a locate investigation. Remember I told you, you may be surprised what you didn't know about your little sister."

"You did," she replied hesitantly.

"Okay. First, do you know anything about property down in Florida?"

"Property in Florida? Hmm...daddy...my father left us some property in Tennessee. You're saying she owns property down in Florida?"

"No, not saying that yet. Couple of addresses coming back to her are in the West Palm Beach area, but the Recorder's Office doesn't show her as owner. What about the condo at Lake Point Tower?"

"Oh God, that mess," Rachel replied. Rachel had tried to talk Annie out of buying the condo with her then boyfriend Will, but young love had a way of short-circuiting certain synapses. She had been only twenty-three, but her modeling career was beginning to bloom, and that meant having too much money she wanted to spend. Will was starting to get some speaking parts in small movies. He came from money though, so despite the fact their skin color was similar, their lives had not been.

"Let me guess. Antoinette and Will were a couple at one time, but that didn't work out?"

"Wow, you are good."

"Not really. That's just reading into behavioral consistencies. She was...twenty-three. Will was twenty-four. Her most recent address is still in the neighborhood; his is out in LA. Does she still stay there sometimes? Rent it out?"

"Both. I mean, she has rented it out. If no one's staying there, she does still crash there sometimes."

"Okay. Good. That's one starting point. David and Lee. She hasn't worked for them in a while, but you know the modeling business. Is it really pretty catty? Would she still be talking to people she may have worked with there?"

"They're no longer in business, but yes, there was a photographer we knew and a couple girls she stayed in touch with. Actually one of them rented the condo."

"You remember her name?"

"Not off hand, but I'll try to. You think it could help?"

"I don't know. Trade secret," he said, leaning back in his chair and looking directly at her. "With locate investigations in general, there are no absolutes. Have to try every available possibility. So, if you can get the name, it might."

"I was thinking of going over to her place anyways."

"She have a diary or journal you could read while you're there? If nothing sudden and unexpected happened to her, there might be something in it."

"Yes. I got her into journaling as early as I could. I think it's a great way to keep yourself honest, along with remembering important big and especially little things."

"I agree. All right. I put a word out to a couple of street sources I have that run from Pilsen to downtown...should hear back in a day or two. Let's meet again on Friday. Let Tim know, if you want him to come with. Meet at Paul's, seven o'clock?"

"Friday, uh, yes...sure, that should be fine." Rachel hoped that Mark hadn't noticed her hesitation. Or at least that he hadn't put any thought to it. She had been looking at the picture of his two boys standing by the canoe, both dressed in jeans and flannel. He had said they were five and six years old, but they were probably more like three and four in that picture. Their SpongeBob life preservers lying at their feet said as much about Mark as it did about them. It made her think of her father, making that crazy Daffy Duck laugh, she and Annie giggling.   *Odd*, she thought and stepped through the door Mark was holding open for her.

***

12:10 p.m.

Rachel sat down at the small butcher block table nestled in the corner of the breakfast nook, looking over the pictures from her sister's last Victoria's Secret shoot. It was odd that the pictures were out and probably meant she had company the last time she was home. Seeing her in the bra and panties, the well-rehearsed, wanting, come-hither expression highlighted by pouty lips and brushed eyebrows, Rachel couldn't stop the feeling of guilt from starting to arise again.

"Where are you, Annie?"

Rachel felt the click in her throat after the words floated in the small apartment for a few seconds and knew that meant the tears were on their way. She didn't want to cry anymore. Tim and Mark both told her to stay away from the guilt, but Tim said she should let the tears come.

"Better than bottling it up to come out some other way," he had said the morning they had met Mark for a late breakfast.

The doorbell put a quick end to her struggle. Maybe this would be someone who could provide some kind of information, know something she didn't. Mark said more than once that finding her was going to be a lot about finding the people who were most recently around her. She hoped Tim was right about how good Mark was. He didn't seem like the kind of person Tim would normally put his faith in. He was not the crisp, precise professional that Tim usually associated with. Rough around the edges and a bit vague about the work

64

he'd been doing for over twenty years. He was right about everything so far though, so answering the door was important. Anyone who knew Annie would not find it unusual that her older sister was answering her door.

"Who is it?" Rachel said into the intercom.

"It's Dre...that you Rachel?"

"Yeah, Dre," Rachel answered. "C'mon up."

She pressed the button to let him in. It would be a relief to talk to Andre. He grew up in the same neighborhood they had and got out in a similar fashion. 69th and Ashland was not the worst place in the city, but staying there could be suffocating. People were trapped by forces beyond their control, by their own demons of hatred for those forces, and the by excuses and rationalizations that hatred allowed.

Andre was also one of the people who moved easily between the music world and the fashion world without seeming predatory. He still wasn't ready to come out yet, and it might be a while before he could risk losing his tough, street rapper brand. He was nowhere near the level of a Kanye or a Jay-Z, but even where he was at, people weren't always understanding. And not having a real partner at the moment, it was not as if he was masking a relationship by constantly being surrounded by Annie and her friends.

"Andre," Rachel said, opening her arms up and letting her heel hold the door.

"Rachel, my little sister," Andre replied, throwing his arms around her. He squeezed her tightly and released. "Now, let me get you one of these muffins I brought with...they are incredible."

"I'll put on some coffee," Rachel replied and turned to walk toward the kitchen.

"Sounds great. Is little sister here, or be back soon?"

"No. Not sure," Rachel called over her shoulder. "Are you primping in front of the mirror?"

"Primping? Oh my, is someone in a bad mood?"

Rachel looked over at Andre as he walked into the kitchen and could see the concern that his comment belied. Part of his on-stage persona was a sort of glaring stare and upturned corner of his lip. Given his darker skin, well-cut muscular build, and shaven head, he pulled off the angry, care-about-nothing look very well. So much of life in front of a camera of any sort was like some kind of acting role, playing into the carefully constructed misconceptions of popular culture.

"Sorry. Did I sound bitchy?"

"Hmm…"

"I did. I guess it's just I'm worried. Haven't heard from Annie since Thursday."

"It's only Tuesday, Rae, not even a week," Andre said and stepped over, placing warm strong hands on her shoulders. "She's a big girl now. And that means she might play a little more than you'd like."

"Andre, I'm not naïve. I know she might have left the party Friday with somebody and woke up in their place Saturday. But even if their place was in another state or on an island, she usually doesn't leave me with nothing for this long…no texts or anything."

Rachel felt Andre's strong hands massaging her shoulders and tried to relax. He knew them both well and understood the lifestyle. Her mind told her that if Andre wasn't worried, there was probably nothing to worry about. It was hard not to. It wasn't like Antoinette to go a day or two without at least texting or tweeting a picture.

"Did you two have some words?"

"Okay, Andre, you can stop being right now. She was talking her line about Tim being just another proper portfolio boyfriend."

"Oh dear," Andre said, his massaging hands hesitating for a moment and then pressing again. "You know, Rae, I try not to be judging in that kind of thing. But, you know it looks like that to her. You've got your life pretty organized, disciplined...she's not like that."

"But she doesn't know Tim."

"Rachel, I'm not saying she's right. But, we both know people can be quick to judge based on little knowing."

"Sorry. I'm just worried."

"Rae, I know you got the mother spot when your mama died, even more so when your dad passed six years ago, but you have to remember yourself at that age. You've done better than most, getting your degree and stepping from one side of the camera to the other. Annie isn't you, though, and she's probably still feeling a little need to step out of your shadow."

"You think?"

"Girl, I know. Could be as simple as she lost her phone and is somewhere with someone and not in a rush to get it replaced. She doesn't have another shoot for a couple weeks, and you know we all need a little 'scape sometimes."

"Yes," Rachel replied, thinking about Tim's down-time weekends. "I guess you're right."

"Look Rae, I just got back from shows up north. I'll do some asking around later today and tomorrow. If it's anything to worry about, we'll know. Now, I think that coffee is ready, and you have got to try one of these caramel apple muffins."

Rachel breathed in deeply and let out a sigh that carried at least some of her tension with it. She knew Andre was right, and she also trusted him to follow through. She stepped over to the cabinet, opened it, and reached for two cups. Between Andre and Mark, she would know if there was really anything to worry about by this time Friday.

***

1:30 p.m.

"Mom, I am sure she's a nice girl, but the boys spend time with their mother, and believe it or don't, I do a fairly good job of taking care of them when they're with me."

"I'm sure you do the best you can, Mark," his mother replied.

Mark held back from responding to the comment. His mother was not different from a lot of women who believed men could be capable of teaching boys baseball, but couldn't teach them much outside of sports and tools. Some of that thinking was generational on her part.

"What are your plans today, Mom?"

"You're just going to avoid the subject then? Mark, when was the last time you did anything besides work and take care of the boys? I don't remember the last time I heard you talk about catching a northern or a Musky from the Fox. I know you love your boys, but even your father needed time to himself—which doesn't mean work time."

"Mom, I love you too. But I told you I was working and might have to get off the phone quick. I have to go—the people I'm watching are moving."

"Hmm...all right, Mark. But please, honey, think about it."

"I will, Mom. Promise. Take care."

Mark put his phone in his pocket and watched as the two men walked out of the lobby of one of the highest of the high end condominium complexes in the city. One of them he was certain he recognized but couldn't remember what from. He thought he was a member of the Justino crew but couldn't be sure. He was family, but Mark couldn't remember for sure which one. Which meant, most likely they both were. They were dressed appropriately: navy blue pin-striped suits, red paisley ties, non-descript black dress shoes. They walked together in a manner that seemed practiced, as if they had been working together for some time, and their movements were synchronized, almost tactical. It was both the blandness of their attire and the fact it was close to matching that caused Mark to try to see if he could get the plate of the black Cadillac that pulled up to them.

"Livery. Figures," Mark said and put his digital voice recorder down.

Whether they had actually ordered a car to pick them up or someone they knew drove, it was not likely the two were at the building for a social visit. Mark took out a cigarette and got out of his car. He lit the cigarette, walked around, and leaned back against the passenger door, keeping his eyes toward the front of the building while his mind sifted through possibilities. Given the people who stayed at Lake Point Towers, it was no surprise to see a couple of guys who looked like family people paying a visit—whether it was Hollywood, New York, or even Nashville, the higher the stakes the greater the likelihood somebody in the mix was owned by one of the families, whether or not they realized it. Was it just coincidence they had been there, and what was the likelihood he could get the doorman or front desk to give him anything about where they might have gone? Two of Antoinette's playmates stayed at the Towers, but that didn't mean they had been there looking for her.

"No shit. Mother fu…" Mark stopped himself from completing the expression. He watched as the all too familiar dark blue Chevy Tahoe slowly rolled up to the lobby entrance. The vehicle would likely not be noticed by most people, and it was definitely not the norm for law enforcement. Mark knew that Robert Tyse would be stepping out of the vehicle in about thirty seconds. Bob, who insisted most people call him Robert, was slow, methodical, and probably one of the few people Mark had known that could fit that avenging angel stereotype some law enforcement were given. He ran for a children's charity, some of the same runs every year. He gave blood almost as frequently as Mark did. But, he was also a three-tour Afghanistan veteran. Marine sniper. When it came to *the shit stops here*, Bob kind of defined it. Whatever he was there about, it would be serious. Just how serious would dictate whether or not he would talk to Mark at all. There had been more than one occasion when Bob had told Mark point blank *you're not on the need to know list.*

If Bob were going into the same place the guidos had just been, it was becoming more likely that Rachel's fears might not be completely unfounded. Lake Point Towers was not immune to regular visits from people at various levels of involvement with the family, but not typically law enforcement like Bob. Bob was not the kind of detective that always made the finest people at city hall happy. He was not the type to comply with anyone's political agenda if it had anything to do with an investigation he was conducting. Mark knew it had cost Bob promotions and other opportunities, but he also knew that it was the standard that they both understood and conducted themselves by. Bob had more than once half-jokingly chided Mark about his unprofessional demeanor and appearance, but that was an unspoken agreement of keeping up popular perceptions. It kept people who might otherwise be curious from seeing anything unusual. Military and other experience they shared taught them both that allowing people their misconceptions could work to your benefit. No one who saw their interactions in public would guess they assisted each other from time to time with investigations.

Mark pinched the end of his cigarette and tossed the butt into the garbage can at the curb. He took another one out, lit it, and leaned back against his car again. He wished he had a cup of coffee because he knew it might be a long time before Bob came out. He was going to try to talk to him because even if Bob didn't say why he was there, Mark wanted to make sure Bob knew the family people had been there.

***

"Detective Robert Tyse," Mark called as he closed the distance to the Tahoe. "What a coincidence."

"Damn, and it seemed like it was going to be such a nice, simple day," Bob said and stopped walking. "I hope for your sake it's merely a coincidence we're both here, detective Hamilton."

"That's what I like about you, Robert," Mark said and stepped closer. "You're always looking out for my best interests."

"Murtaugh, Riggs," Bob said, turning to face the two uniformed officers who arrived after Tyse. "I'm going to 25 for a few minutes with the shylock here. Why don't you go grab a coffee and a smoke."

The two younger officers looked at Bob, then at Mark, then back at Bob. The white officer pointed at the black one and then feigned holding a joint tightly pinched between his thumb and forefinger and taking a hit. Mark smiled. Despite the fact he let very few people know it, Bob actually had a pretty good sense of humor. The black officer then made a hand gesture as if he were stroking himself and hooked the thumb of the other hand at the white officer. Mark chuckled and noticed that Bob hesitated a second, a slight upturn in the corner of his mouth.

"Riggs," Bob shouted. "Save your crude attempts at humor for when you're not in uniform representing the city."

"Yes, sir."

"And don't call me 'sir.' I work for a living."

"Nice touch," Mark said and watched as the two young officers walked away.

"Okay, Mark," Bob said and waved a hand held low in a motion away from the front of the building. "Hold your chatter for a minute."

Mark followed Bob as he walked away from the front entrance of the building. Mark knew that Bob specifically used the word chatter to let him know the information he had was serious. With their shared military background, it was understood *hold your chatter* was a phrase used when you wanted it clear that communications might be worth listening to or were being listened to. In the military it meant ceasing radio communications; in this case, Mark knew it meant Bob was clearly indicating that this was serious enough he didn't want to risk the young officers or anyone close by overhearing their conversation.

"All right, Mark. No disrespect, but this is how this is going to work. I'm going to ask you give me at least some general idea of what you're working on. If there are any parallels to why I'm here, I'll give you what I can, which won't be much."

"Yeah, thanks, I'm good, Bob. How's Stephanie and little Robbie?"

"Cute, Mark. They're good, thanks for asking. Look, I just have to be quick here. Tell me what you're doing in Crook County and especially at Lake Pointe."

"Got a client with a missing sister. Early twenties, modeling business, owns a unit up in the building."

"Shit. Please tell me she's not bi-racial with an older sister, no parents living."

"Will you tell me more if I say she's not?"

"You are a clever one, Mark. Damn it, this is serious, but right now I don't even know for sure what it is. I won't ask you who your client is, but if it's the sister, you best do a good job of keeping a close eye on her too…Justino family may be involved."

"That would explain the guidos who left just as you got here."

"What? Really? You recognize either of them?"

"One of them, yeah. Could pick him out of a book if you need me too. You really don't know what you're looking for?"

"Going to tell you more than I should for your client's sake. The sister filed an information report, but nothing for anyone to do because the subject's not a minor. Few days later, couple sources I got down at Alligator Records tell me that there's been a soft push from Justino people to find this girl. Nothing about bad business, just they want to talk to her handlers about something, and they're keeping the chatter above the streets—they're not trusting their streetside people to keep it quiet. You have any reason to believe she slipped over to the shady side?"

"I didn't. Going to have to ask my client to go through her sister's place thoroughly."

"Good idea, Mark. Meet me down at Grand Central around 5. Should have a couple things back by then. Keep me posted as you go, and I'll give you what I can."

"Ten-four, Bob."

As Mark walked away and back toward his car, he made a mental note to put together a list of Antoinette's friends for Bob so he could cross reference the names with anything he might have with current Justino activity. If any of them were involved with that family, they were as likely to know something as anyone else. As the saying went, with friends like that, who needs enemies? But, using their legally restricted methods, it might be a while before Bob could put together the information. Information was always one of the cross sections where private detectives and law enforcement could assist each other to mutual benefit, if proper respect was allowed. Different restrictions, regulations, and sources, each with their own variable reliability.

Mark looked back at the tall, elegant building that was Lake Pointe Towers. He would come back another day if necessary. Between the guidos and Bob, it was not likely anyone there was going to be amenable to a private detective, even if cash were involved. Even those who had no idea what it was all about would be protecting the management and tenants, as they were trained to do. People who lived in places like Lake Point needed to be protected, whether it was from the paparazzi or the police.

***

3:30 p.m.

"I was up in Wisconsin that weekend, Edward," Tim said and turned around to face his ex-partner. Edward Rossi stared at Tim, and Tim recognized that stare. Edward did not give a shit. To Edward, Tim was just a lost cause, recovering alcoholic who was lucky to be alive. Standing in his 180 North LaSalle office, king of his little fashion empire, Edward probably didn't even understand how completely replaceable he was to the family. "I have no idea what happened or what was going on at that party. I just told Rachel I would ask attorneys I knew who were involved with the fashion business. I'm just trying to help Rachel—her sister's missing. I'm not trying to cause trouble for anyone. Rachel has no idea of my life before...before I got sick."

"Tim, what the hell did you think my response was going to be? 'Sure Tim, you used to be with us; I'll give you a fucking list of the attendees'?. Fucking Christ. Tim, you weren't born yesterday. Still not sure why Don Justino let you walk, but I'm going to do you one favor. One, and hopefully you'll listen carefully. Are you listening carefully, Tim?"

"Yes, Edward," Tim replied hesitantly, closing his eyes and wishing he were anywhere but here. It was demeaning. This little Napoleon who couldn't understand why Don Justino let him walk was talking down to him, and because of his...because of his health problems, Edward Rossi was in, and he was out. "I'm listening."

"I'm not going to say a word to anyone. I'm not going to ask a single person a single fucking question. Okay, you listened. Do you fucking understand?"

Tim hesitated for a moment. He was staring at Edward Rossi and not seeing him at all. He was seeing Richard Kingston. Richard Kingston, who had invited him to the party his senior year in high school. Richard Kingston, who had cost him his standing in his class and the respect of his father. Tim clenched his right hand, nails digging into flesh. Rossi was lucky it was broad daylight and his secretary was in the other room. If it were not for that, he'd learn what Richard Kingston knew about the fragility of the windpipe.

"I understand, Edward."

"Now, get the hell out of my office."

Tim's fingernails dug deeper into the palms of his right hand. He was in control. He would not embarrass himself, his family, or those close to him. He was recovering. He was giving it over. He was not strong enough to do it on his own. He would confess his weakness, his wrongdoings to his father. He would acknowledge he needed his father's help. Acknowledge the blackjack and the strap kept him in check, reminded him of his weak human flesh. He looked over at Edward Rossi as he opened the door to the office. The Italians and their judgmental Catholicism. Judgment was the worst addiction.

"What? You got something else?"

"No, no Edward," Tim replied. His right hand unclenched, and he smiled. "Sorry to bother you."

Tim walked out of the office and past Edward's secretary, wishing her a good day. He looked at his watch. Almost four-thirty. He needed to talk to Connelly and Gianconno but had a five o'clock appointment about a contract with Alligator. He noticed as his hand reached out to the elevator button that he needed to fit a manicure into his schedule somewhere tomorrow. *So many things to do*, he told himself. Telling Rachel he wasn't getting anywhere could wait. As he stepped onto the elevator, Tim tried to remember if he had dropped off the dry cleaning. Cleanliness, after all, was next to godliness.

***

5:15 p.m.

"Yes, he's a private detective," Bob said, waving for Mark to step into the hallway past the uniformed officer who had been detaining him. "But they're not all like Bert Ratso. Ratso dresses a lot better than Detective Hamilton, but Detective Hamilton just can't remember he's not under anymore."

"Thanks, Bob," Mark said, looking back at the young police officer, wondering if he was even seasoned enough to know the reference to being undercover. "Always count on you for moral support."

"I'm all about the warm and fuzzy, Mark. You know that."

"Yeah, I can see you've got people here mesmerized," Mark returned and followed Bob into his office. "Where is everyone anyways? Vincenzo and McGavin were the only two I saw still at their desks."

"Everyone else has a work ethic. We actually have to go out and work for our information," Bob said loudly and closed the door as Mark walked in.

"Damn boss," Mark said. He walked over to Mark's desk, sat down, and put his feet up. "You don't want to maybe think about taking some of that sensitivity training the department offers?"

"In rare form tonight, Mark?"

"We always bring out the best in each other, right, Bob?"

"All right, asshole," Bob joked, a grin growing at the corners of his mouth. "The door is closed now."

"We do have our fun though."

77

"You gonna take your shoes off my desk?"

"Oh, sorry. Got kinda comfortable there for a minute."

Mark took his feet off the desk and sat up. He took his notebook and case file out from under his arm and opened up the file. He pulled a section of the report out and leaned over, placing the papers in front of Bob. He waited a moment for Bob to look at the report before speaking.

"Not sure what might be useful to you. Will Washington was originally on the condo at Lake Pointe with her. Giselle Harris was the last person to rent it from Antoinette. Antoinette's last shoot was for Victoria's Secret. She currently works through Martha's. No boyfriend for the last three months...no one steady anyways. Did some work for a band signed with Alligator. Any of that good?"

"Mark, you know how much legwork you just saved me and my people? We don't have that much for you. Contacts say that Justino's people are looking to talk to her handlers, which means they think she's still alive. None of the street sources have heard anything about a flare up between families, or families and any of the gangs."

"There was a party last weekend. Big modeling thing. She was supposed to be there. Supposed to have gone down in one of the old warehouses near Pilsen."

"Yeah, they still use them sometimes. Like the days of raves. Nice when you can bring a party to a location where everything can be cleaned up and disappeared twenty-four hours later."

"Harder to track down though."

"I have a pretty good relationship with Connelly and Gianconno. Of course, they never tell you everything, but they know when a line has been crossed. I'll check with them tomorrow. Take a look through this; see if you recognize the gentlemen from Lake Pointe."

"Okay," Mark said, taking the unmarked binder from Bob. He leafed through the assortment of pictures and reports. It appeared to be thrown together haphazardly, which Mark knew meant that Bob had done it himself. Bob trusted almost no one, not even some of the people he worked with. Often that meant he did not want his path or direction known to anyone going through his desk or office. "Got him."

"Let's see," Bob said and reached to take the binder from Mark. "Okay. Good and bad. That's one of Michael DiNino's people."

"Meaning?"

"Michael is one of their front people. Has meetings with the mayor and other people. If Michael's looking for someone, it has nothing to do with business as usual in their world but trying to keep business as usual going strong in the regular world. They may just want to get her more secured with one of their agencies."

"Okay. I got a text from one of my snitches on the way over. Stays in the Pilsen neighborhood, not too far from the warehouse they tricked out for the party. Never know what you're going to hear, but Amber's been pretty reliable."

"Not leaving anything on voicemail though, so try maybe answering your phone once or twice tomorrow."

"Try calling from the same phone once or twice."

"One more thing, Mark," Bob said and paused for a moment looking around. "You know what, get it to you in a little bit."

"Not like that 'call you in ten' from the McGhee case?"

"All right, wise guy," Bob said, stood up, walked over to the door, and opened it. "I think that's enough of my time for one night. You can tell me the rest on the way out."

"Ten four, Officer Friendly," Mark responded and stepped out of Bob's office, holding the door for him. "Maybe I can get you a cup of coffee and a donut."

"I know, I know. Private detectives have pastries; cops have doughnuts."

As they walked out of what they affectionately referred to as Grand Central station, they continued their banter. Once outside, they looked at each other, smiled, and laughed softly. Mark knew that their act was something they both enjoyed. You didn't experience twenty years of police or private detective work without seeing enough of life that you could laugh at most anything, including yourself. As they reached the street, they shook hands and went their different directions. Mark was glad to hear that Rachel's sister was likely alive and well. When they went through her condo the next day, hopefully they'd find something about a boyfriend or weekend away she had just not wanted to tell Rachel.

* * *

6:45 p.m.

Fred didn't recognize the white guy wearing the jean jacket and woven pony-tail that Tyse had been talking to as he watched them walk out of Grand Central station; probably DEA given that hippie kind of look. He knew Detective Bob Tyse. Tyse had taken down the Hernandez operation. Sure, the Feebies liked to talk about how they and the Justice Department were responsible. But they wouldn't have gotten anywhere without Tyse's guidance. The Justino family wasn't involved in that heroin operation, but the arrests gave

80

everyone in the community notice that Tyse was hard to shake. Tyse was the kind of cop who was fine with the Fed getting the credit though. Let other people take the headlines. He was a tough son of a bitch, but he was a straight shooter. Certain people you had to respect and let go about their business. The Justino family had the right people in the right places, so Tyse would never get too close. And as good as he was, he may even have recognized that he was taking care of the competition. But then, a man has to know his limitations.

Fred waited until they had pulled away and then got out of his car. He walked quickly across Western Avenue, knowing how unpredictable drivers could be in the area. He stepped into the front lobby and quickly scanned to see if he recognized any of the officers hanging around. Most of the ones in uniform were too young to have a clue, and the only plain-clothed officers were dressed as if they had spent all day in court. Fred stepped up to the front glass.

"May I help you, sir?"

"I'm here to see Detective Vincenzo, thank you, Sergeant," Fred replied. Fred had never been in the military, but he thought that police probably liked having their rank acknowledged the same way that people in the military did. Fred remembered his two cousins who had been in the Army talking about how good it felt to be recognized as a non-commissioned officer.

"He's expecting you, sir?"

"Yes."

"Have a seat, sir. I'll call him, and he'll be right out."

"Thank you, Sergeant." Fred looked around the waiting area again and then sat down on the bench, pressing his back up against the wall. He looked at his watch. He was ten minutes early. Something he had learned long ago: Always be at least ten minutes early for any work-related meetings—it could often give you a tactical edge. Fred heard a door open just to his right and looked up.

"Fred, you still wearing your watch upside down?"

"Detective Vincenzo, it's not upside down; it's just in the right place," Fred replied. That had been their customary greeting for at least the last ten years. Fred always wore the face of his watch on the bottom side of his wrist, making checking the time easier and the likelihood of spilling a drink to do so lessened. "You still carrying that old wheel gun?"

"Fred, if it takes more than six, I better not be alone."

They hugged briefly and walked back into the offices of the police station. As they walked down the hallway, Fred couldn't help but notice how much things really stayed the same. Instead of Chicago mobsters, the Chicago Crime Commission was now identifying gang members for everybody, trying to convince themselves, as well as anyone who would listen, that Chicago government was above and beyond their influence.

As they stepped into Vincenzo's office, Fred stepped immediately to his right, next to a row of filing cabinets, out of the line of sight of most people in the surrounding offices and hallway. Always best to take every precaution that eliminated a possibility of an unexpected, chance identification. Fred very rarely was known to many of the street level workers, but you didn't stay in the business for over twenty years without having some contacts.

"Antonio, how's Marie? The twins?"

"They're good, Fred. Thank you for asking. One of the things I like about you, Fred, you remember people. The boys are graduating high school this year. One going to play football at Nebraska, the other attending friggin' Columbia College. Multi-media something. Marie's boy, that one."

"Geez, Antonio. Let the boy do what he wants. Could be worse: could be going to law school."

Vincenzo smiled and they both chuckled lightly. With the exception of perhaps lobbyists, lawyers were the least respected profession among most of the family Fred knew. They were necessary, and some of them even could be said to do good work, but Fred had yet to meet one who would stand up for what they supposedly believed in outside the courtroom, even the ones who worked for the family.

"Lawyers, guns, and money, eh Fred?"

"Right," Fred replied, enjoying the reference to the Warren Zevon song.

"But I know you came to talk about something important, Fred. What can I do for you?"

"Thank you, Antonio. I just have a few questions. Have to do with one of your areas. There was a party last weekend, big one with some of the modeling people. I heard that Michael DiNino was there looking for a girl. Do you know anything about that? Do you know anything about the girl?"

"Fred, all I know is what little Michael told me. They're not looking for the girl herself. They want to talk to her people. They want her at an event, but they don't want her to know they have anything to do with her being there."

"An event? What does that mean, Antonio, an event? The Justino family doesn't exactly have company picnics out at the forest preserve."

"Fred," Antonio replied, smiling and chuckling. "You always say shit like that. You are funny. I don't know what kind of—what they mean by an event."

"But they are keeping it off the street Just talking to their go-betweens with her people?"

"Right. Exactly. You know how it works, Fred."

"I do." Fred replied, flashed a smile, and then sat back in his chair. Antonio knew something more. He changed his sentence in mid-stream, which meant he wanted to word it a particular way, which meant there was a lie in there somewhere. Fred knew that someone told him to lie, and he knew sometimes you let things go; sometimes it was better not to call people out and press. They were keeping off the street, and that meant there was no intention of taking action against the girl. And, Fred thought, that meant this was one of those times when there was a left field, a wild card. Whatever happened, it had nothing to do with family business.

"You okay, Fred?"

"I'm good, Antonio. Thank you for your help."

"That's it?"

"That's it. Now, you have work to do, and so do I. Hopefully I'll see one son playing for the Bears and maybe the other broadcasting the game, eh? You stay here, I'll let myself out—you know, being seen together too much..."

"I know, Fred."

They hugged briefly, and Fred patted Vincenzo on the back to let him know all was well between them. Antonio was doing his job, and Fred would not hold that against him. Now though, he had to rely on Bert Ratso. Ratso was reliable but not trustworthy. Not many people understood the world of difference between those two words. Fred knew it was his best bet for being able to get a quick answer without going directly to the Don. Going directly to the Don about something that did not have to do with their business was unusual. Fred knew his limits with the Don very clearly. This would not create much difficulty. Don Justino might yell a little, might curse at Fred, but that would be the worst of it. He knew Fred's loyalty was beyond question.

CHAPTER FOUR

Wednesday, June 22nd
9:30 am

Mark waited for the convertible BMW to pull out of the spot near the corner of Irving Park and Lake Shore Drive. Parallel parking was a lost art out in the suburbs, but Mark proved he hadn't lost his touch by pulling just past the now open spot, and backing quickly, whipping the wheel so it seemed he almost slid into the space.

Rachel had access to the underground parking for the condo building at Irving Park and Lake Shore Drive, so he wasn't going to wait in the car for her to show up. On the other hand, he thought as he looked at his watch, it was not likely she, like Mark always was, would be fifteen minutes early.

"Sorry, Terry," Mark said as he turned off the car radio, cutting off the interview in progress. There were times he would sit for a few extra minutes to hear Terry Gross interview someone, but not today. Yet another *New York Times* Best Selling Author was not someone Mark felt intrigued by. "It's all been done before."

Mark's eyes scanned the streets. Although he lived out in Elgin, he had lived in the city for several years and knew it well as a result of working investigations from criminal defense to adoption searches. There were times he missed the city. Being able to get up at 5:00 a.m., run along the lakeshore, and know that there was a coffee shop, restaurant, or store that was open within walking distance was something that he missed.

He walked around the corner to the front of the building and sat down on the front steps. He pulled a cigarette out of the pack in his chest pocket, lit it, took a deep inhale, and watched the group of twenty-somethings across the street, walking along the bike path.

In college, he had lived off 18th and Halsted, a rough and tumble, blue collar neighborhood very different from this one. No one in the neighborhood at that time, except the gangsters higher up in the hierarchy, was driving a convertible BMW. He did not need a car, and he enjoyed being able to get anywhere without having to drive. He could get down to Maxwell street for a polish and some slightly damaged but new-in-the-box merchandise, manufacturer's warranty not available. That was Maxwell street before the University and city took it upon themselves to improve the neighborhood, the way it was when featured in the Blues Brothers. He could get down to the museum campus or to Little Italy for a real sub from the deli inside the grocery store at Fontano's—fresh baked breads and nothing pre-made.

Mark crushed his cigarette out and noticed a group of runners on the bike path across the drive. If their high and tights and lean, muscular bodies didn't give them away, the *ARMY* emblazoned across their grey running shirts left no room for doubt. Mark smiled, thinking about running in the desert as the gorgeous sunset filled the horizon over the mountains. Orange-yellow fading up to a reddish that gave way to darker blue into purple before reaching the black of night. His tour had been mostly a good one. Working AWOL Apprehension, chasing down AWOL and Deserter status soldiers, had helped to hone some of his skills for locating people.   Being part of the Special Reactions Team had provided him the opportunity to become familiar with some exotic weaponry, and he was one of a few people on the team that had become adept at Australian repelling—bouncing down the side of a building face forward. Although the team had only been called out once to a real incident, standing by in support of the local law enforcement S.W.A.T.in the midst of a hostage crisis, even the training alerts were pretty intense. He had only deployed overseas for six months, part of a special interrogations unit attached to the C.I.D. That experience had been a large part of what informed his decision to get out after his first tour. *Platoon* had spoken to what front line combat could do to the souls of men, but seeing the atrocities being committed away from live fire was, for Mark, even worse.   Even the most neophyte interrogator knew that confessions and information obtained through torture were of questionable value.

As the young troops rounded the curve and faded out of sight, Mark looked at his watch. He still wore it with the face on the underside of his right wrist, a habit learned from Staff Sergeant Rick Hanes, the Assistant N.C.OI.C. of both the AWOL Apprehension Team and the S.R.T. Rick was probably the only person besides Bob that Mark felt he would never want to cross. At 240 lean, muscular pounds, the Kentucky boy, as he used to refer to himself, had become skilled at 6 different martial arts disciplines. Someone who was that big and could move that quickly and smoothly was scary or impressive, depending upon which side of his list you were on.

"Hmm…perhaps they did get here early," Mark said. And, he thought, that made sense with Rachel growing more anxious about her sister. Rachel was not happy to hear about the possibility of an organized crime connection but was not completely surprised either. She knew the business and the possibilities and immediately understood and agreed to let Mark toss the apartment for any kind of information or indication that would clarify the question. Mark told her that listening devices were much more sophisticated in the last ten years, but that many were still discoverable if you knew what to look for and where.

Mark opened the heavy glass door and walked into the small, glass lobby cubicle where the directory and buzzers for the apartment were. He scrolled through the list on the digital display and found Rachel's extension. He dialed it and instinctively stepped back. There was a high-pitched squawk, a moment of fuzz, and then ringing.

"Who is it?" a deeply bass voice, sounding angry, asked through the crackling of the intercom system.

Mark hesitated for a moment. Not hearing Rachel's voice would have been one thing, but that was definitely not Tim's voice either. And if anyone was at Antoinette's condo other than Rachel, it could be somebody who had answers. Some of the people who had those answers might not be the friendly talkative type, and the voice that came through sounded a lot like angry street people he had met over the years, angry being a state that they lived in rather than anything having to do with the immediate circumstances. On the other hand, Mark thought, he could have just dialed the wrong number. He looked at the panel and was careful to be certain he dialed correctly.

"Said, *who is it?* Y'all playin' some kinda game?"

"Hello," Mark answered quickly. "I'm here to meet with Antoinette."

"Oh you is? Well come on up. Thought you was gonna make me hafta come down, holla at you or somethin'."

"She's up there?"

"I said, come on up, right?"

"Right," Mark answered, reaching over to grab the polished metal door handle as he heard the muffled click of the door unlocking.

As he walked over to the elevators, Mark reminded himself that voices do not always reflect the stature of the person. That deeply bass voice could as easily belong to someone as short and thin as John Legend as it could to someone as tall and thick as Barry White. Mark did not like taking unnecessary chances though, so as one hand reached to press the button for the seventh floor, the other was checking to make sure the steel baton he liked to carry was in this jacket and not his leather. As the elevator doors closed, Mark tilted his head down, closed his eyes, and exhaled deeply.

***

Mark stood just to the left of the door, his body at a forty-five degree angle. His right hand held the extended baton so that it ran along the outside line of his right leg. His left hand reached out and knocked hard on the door twice. His right hand tightened on the baton, and his torso twisted slightly back and to the right, solidifying his center of balance.

"What you playin', fool?" Andre shouted as he opened the door slightly, pulling it close to his chest, leaving Mark only a sliver of his shoulder exposed.

"Ask you the same," Mark answered and thrust the baton out in front of him, across the line of the open doorway, pivoting and jamming his foot at the base of the doorway, preventing the door from being closed. He thrust the weight of his body into the baton, pushing the door closed against Andre, and pivoted again. Both arms came up, pushing the door harder against Andre.

"Fuck you, little man!" Andre shouted and rolled his shoulder into the door, one foot pushing off the wall, pressing his full force and weight against the door.

Mark jammed the baton between the closing door and the wall, stepped back quickly, and delivered a strong snap kick to the bottom of the door, hoping to surprise the big man and perhaps catch his knees. The response of "mothafucker" was what Mark hoped to hear, and he seized the second of hesitation, yanking the door back and popping it back at the large man. He didn't wait for a reaction but spun into the condo, the baton held out in front of him.

"What the hell is going on?" Rachel shouted.

Mark turned to look. A second after he saw Rachel standing in the hallway from the bathroom, wrapped in a towel, her hair still wet, he felt Andre's hand on his chest, slamming him back against the wall. The strong hand moved up to his neck and held him pinned.

"Andre! Mark! Would you two heroes stop saving me?"

Mark looked at the tall, muscular black man who looked like he was stiff-arming someone on the football field. Their eyes met, and their bodies relaxed. Mark dropped the baton and slid down to a crouching position; his hand moved to rub his throat. He was certain what Rachel was about to say.

"Andre, meet Mark Hamilton, private detective. Mark, meet Andre Johnson, longtime friend of mine and Annie's."

Mark looked at Andre and couldn't stop the embarrassed smile from growing. Andre looked like he was at least five foot ten and a solid two hundred twenty-five pounds. The same smile started to show across Andre's face, and he shook his head, laughing. Mark let the laugh come as well, nervous energy dissipating.

"Now, would one of you close the door so not everyone gets a free view?" Rachel said and turned to walk back to the bathroom. "Men. Andre, take Mark to the kitchen, and I think we'll want some coffee. Mark, you can talk openly to Andre; he knows most everything about my life and Annie's."

"Got it, Rae," Andre replied and offered Mark a hand.

"Nice to meet you, Andre," Mark said and allowed the strong hand to help him up.

"Pleasure's all mine, Mark."

They looked at each other again, grinning and shaking their heads. Mark tried to think if Rachel mentioned that someone would be with her. He hoped he was remembering correctly that she didn't. He could save a little face. He watched as Andre walked to the kitchen and noticed as Andre got closer to the refrigerator that his shoulders seemed to relax, and the big man's movement shifted from the stereotypical, arms-out body builder. Andre opened the refrigerator door, and Mark saw the picture of Andre, his head resting on another man's chest. For a moment, he was tempted to make a joking remark about the cliché of a model having gay men around her but thought perhaps it was not the right moment. Maybe later, if either of them actually said anything about Andre being gay.

***

"It's a fine line, Mark," Rachel said, handing Mark another stack of papers from the bottom drawer of the small, wooden filing cabinet. "We all walk it to some degree at some point in our lives. Some of us, like Andre, more than others."

Mark looked over at Andre. Andre was seated at the small kitchen table, busy going over two journals that Rachel had discovered under a large photo album in a drawer of the nightstand in Annie's bedroom. The way he held his chin cupped in his hand and his posture were so stereotypically gay, an observation which Mark felt awkward about. He had played the gay part more than once in his career in order to get information or effectuate service of process. He had even lectured about the use of such stereotypes as effective tools because most of society operated from a sort of belief in them. It was odd to know that, while you understood something as being inherently wrong, sometimes you used even other people's lazy misconceptions to your advantage— indirectly continuing or perhaps even furthering them.

"I do understand, Rachel. The world and its trouble with the other."

"I don't know, Mark. No offense, but it's hard for a straight, white man who came from an intact family to truly understand. Intellectually, yes. But to really, in your heart, know what it's like? I don't know."

"Hmm," Mark responded and glanced over the bills and letters. He knew Rachel was right on one level. He would never really know what it was like to be black or gay in America, much less both. But, operating outside the accepted societal norms wasn't encapsulated in being one of those two things. *That's for another day*, Mark thought and looked back at the papers. The bills all seemed quite normal, and most of the letters were either junk mail or old ones from Will. Mark couldn't help but wonder if he had missed something when he read over Will's background report. "I'm not finding anything here. Andre, any interesting reading there?"

"Oh, you know, Mark. Just the kind of things you'd rather not know about a girl, even though we all know we're the same in ways."

"Naughty bits, eh?" Mark joked, pretending a British accent.

"Naughty vicar," Andre replied, adding his own version of a British accent. "Friends can be just like family—pictures you don't want in your head."

"Not of my baby sister, you don't."

There was a second of silence, and then they all laughed. Mark stood up and stretched, and then glanced over at Rachel, still going through the rest of the papers. For a moment, he was distracted by her small but full bottom lip and the smoothness of her skin. She was a strong, intelligent woman. He quickly dismissed the thoughts. She was unquestionably an attractive woman, but she was also his client. His client who lived in a different world, a world of BMWs and Mercedes, not Nissans and Toyotas. And, he reminded himself, she was involved with Tim.

"Andre," Mark said and stepped over to where Andre was seated. "You know people in both the modeling and music worlds; think you could get me to anyone you think might know Annie's movements at least some of that weekend?"

"It would be my pleasure, Mark."

"Careful, Mark," Rachel joked. "I think Andre may mean that."

"Rachel," Andre admonished loudly. "Now, why would you go and say something like that? Damn, girl."

"Because you're maybe the world's biggest flirt."

"Well, I have to admit he is kind of cute. Could have fun with some of the nasty boys down at Alligator. Maybe even make Lucius jealous."

"I thought you were done with Lucius, Andre."

"Rae, you know I can't just walk away. We went out for dinner last week, and he was being so nice."

"Okay," Mark said, putting the papers he was holding down on the table. "Mark is still in the room. Andre, I'm flattered. I'm also very straight. But, I know the way mirroring works. I wouldn't mind playing along, but the important question is, do you think we'd get any more or better information if people thought I was someone from the community?"

"The *community*. Oooh, now it sounds like a spy story," Andre said, smiled, and put down the journal he was reading. "Bless your heart, Mark. No, no I don't. This is about finding Annie. Might even make some people less likely to tell you anything. It's some people there, you can tell they don't mind making money from my talent, but they're thinking I'm devil's work and all that hate stuff—good Christians, you know. And, anyway, Lucius gets jealous if I talk to the waiter too long."

"So, what do you think, Mark?"

"Rachel," Mark said and stood up. He needed to move while his mind was processing bits of information. "I think we have nothing here, which is good news. Hopefully, it means Annie didn't know what was going on around her—maybe got herself involved with somebody she didn't know enough about. Still could be dangerous, but not as bad."

"So, where do we go now?" Rachel asked, stood up, and walked over to the kitchen.

"Well, some clichés exist for a reason. *I have a cop friend*, said the private detective. Actually grew up on the gritty South Side too—Englewood though, 76th and Vincennes. Works homicide and some special units. We help each other from time to time."

"I thought the police wouldn't get involved?"

"Unofficially," Mark lied. He wanted to keep his word to Bob, and he also didn't want to upset Rachel unnecessarily. At this point, they didn't know enough to draw any conclusions. "He's not working this as a homicide; he's just getting some information for me that might take longer for me to access."

"Why would he do it, though?" Rachel asked. "What's in it for him?

"All the arrests and publicity if I turn anything up. It really does work for both of us. I don't want the publicity for a few reasons. He doesn't really want the publicity either; he wants the arrests. He has to be a bit more of a realist though—his bosses want the publicity, want people to see the work that's being done. I get paid the same either way, and for me, overall, my name catching people's attention is not necessarily a good thing.

"You know, Rae," Andre said, "As much as I hate to say it, sometimes a brother asking questions gets some different answers than paleface asking."

"Keepin' it real, Andre," Rachel said and gave him a gentle hug. "Okay, what else Mark? Anything else we can do?"

"Not sure," Mark replied. "I have to meet with someone later today who might have some information. Might not be until tonight, though. Andre, check around; see if there's anyone worth talking to. Rachel, maybe talk to Tim. See if he knows anyone I could talk to."

"I'll try, Mark. Tim's been hard to get hold of the last two days. He said he checked with a couple people. I know he had a couple big contracts up this week."

"All right. Well, thoughts and prayers are always good. I'll see if I can follow up on Will. You never know."

"Very true," Andre said, "Sometimes those flames just go to low ember."

"Not that most men would admit that," Mark replied.

"Well, not straight men anyways."

They all looked at each other and smiled, then laughed. Mark knew, for Rachel especially, a good laugh would help right now. As much as he wanted to believe the appearance of things, he felt something nagging at the back of his mind, telling him all was not right. For now, though, putting that kind of feeling out there without explanation was unnecessary. For now, they just needed to keep doing what they were doing.

* * *

10:30 a.m.

"What the hell, Tim?" Sal Gianconno said and walked over to Tim, placing his hand on Tim's shoulder.

Tim cringed, wanting to slap the hand off his shoulder. Salvatore and his partner Thomas were both the kind of godless people whom Don Justino allowed to run his businesses far too often. No respect and understanding for the underlying order of things, for the necessity of maintaining standards of behavior, of knowing that their sense of control was false and inflated. The hand on his shoulder was an insulting attempt to display control.

"Thomas," Tim said, ignoring Salvatore's non-question. "I'm only asking because my girlfriend is worried about her sister. I'm not inquiring about details or any other information."

"Salvatore," Tom Connelly said, the mocking tone in his voice drippingly obvious. "Can't you see Tim is only worried about his girlfriend? Have you no sense of humanity?"

Humanity, Tim thought. Oh they were both possessed of plenty of humanity. The worst of humanity. Of the weaknesses, of the indulgence of the flesh, of the belief that some trivial, occasional display of remorse at a service on Sunday made a difference. The perhaps annual visit to a booth where Hail Marys and Our Fathers would be required to be repeated, perhaps a few hours of community service. They didn't know work or real discipline.

"Look, Tim," Sal said and stepped back around to his desk. "Believe it or don't, I actually kinda understand where you're coming from. Just need to see what you'd do if I got on you a little."

"Understandable, Salvatore."

"Okay, Tim, call me Sal if you're going to be talking to me and asking favors."

"As you wish."

"As I wish, geez. Tim, I can't tell you who was there or not. We service our clients. Cameras were not on because it was not one of our sites. You want information, you have to talk to the top modeling people. You know who they are."

"And," Tom added, "I'm not sure what's made Sal feel so generous, but I respect he has his reasons. I, on the other hand, think it's very important for you to remember you walked away. So, cross a line and you know what happens.

Ask your questions where you want, but do so carefully. You understand?"

Tim's eyes went from Sal to Tom, and his right hand, which had been resting on the side of his right thigh, began to clench and squeeze. The little man's green eyes stared into his, trying to communicate a threat, a control over him. He returned and held the stare, fingers digging into his thigh. For a moment, he felt his upper body moving forward and relaxed his hand. Not now.

"You understand, Tim?" Sal said.

"I understand, Salvatore. I'll make any inquiries without reference to anyone in the organization, or as if I have an understanding. That should suffice."

"Geez, lawyer through and through, Sal."

"Yeah, Tim definitely has uptight mouthpiece down to a science."

"Right down to that wool dress coat. That's not the same coat, is it, Tim?"

Tim looked down at the coat, folded over on his lap. The Merino coat was the same calf-length style he had worn for over twenty years. It was not the kind of high end, exclusive attire people like Thomas and Salvatore would wear. It had style, but it had function and durability. Even Rachel sometimes seemed to fall prey to the temptation of spending excessively on clothes that did little more than decorate and draw attention to the outer person.

"No, Thomas."

"Okay, we got work to do, Tim. You know the way out."

"Indeed."

Tim got up and walked out without saying another word. He would be able to tell Rachel he talked to everyone he knew. It was enough for now. It was hard, though. It was getting harder. A taste of gin might help to get things back in order. Might help him understand what he had done. None of these people would understand. Rachel herself couldn't really understand. As beautiful as she was, as much as she understood the necessity of discipline, she could be more like Mark at times. Talking about peace and gratitude in idealistic vagaries that avoided work and discipline, that allowed people to recognize their weaknesses without understanding the need to exorcize them.

He hit the elevator call button and closed his eyes for a moment. A cigarette would help. It would help him keep his thoughts focused. Perhaps stop at home. Rest for a little bit. Get away from this world he was not a part of. He heard the ding of the elevator's arrival and opened his eyes. Tim recognized, despite his attire, that the large, muscular black man getting off the elevator was most assuredly law enforcement, and, as he stepped off and turned toward the offices, Tim saw his jacket move slightly, gun and badge revealed. Tim smiled and stepped onto the elevator. Perhaps he would give Salvatore and Thomas at least a bit of earthly fear.

***

7:20 p.m.

Fred pulled into the small lot for the strip that consisted of a payday loan store, a pawn shop, a hole-in-the-wall Mexican eatery, and the offices of Bert A. Ratso, Licensed Private Detective, Protection Specialist. Available, of course, twenty-four/seven. *A class A private detective agency*, declared an ad in bold and italics on the bench near the entrance of the building. The strip was not unusual for the area. Just off Irving Park at Harlem, the neighborhood was on the edge of the city and still predominantly working class. Norridge, Harwood Heights, and the rest of the immediate area were among the few areas that were not greatly in transition. Despite the impact of the recession, these were families that were not being uprooted, people who were picking up a part time job on the overnight shift so they could make their mortgage payments. Fred liked these kinds of neighborhoods, even if he didn't like the kind of businessmen who preyed upon the lack of education of many of its inhabitants.

"Yeah, Bert, you're class A all right," Fred said, backing his car into a spot close to the entrance. Fred knew from doing his own homework that class A was the only type of license issued. Because most people didn't know that, however, less scrupulous people tried to use it as a distinguishing feature in their marketing. At one time, Fred had thought perhaps being a private detective would be a good cover job, but then he realized even people like Bert Ratso had to make friendly with law enforcement.

Fred scanned the lot and the neighboring lot as well before getting out of the car. It never paid to get too comfortable, and Bert Ratso was definitely not someone you trusted your life with. He opened the car door and got out quickly, all his movements short and rehearsed, from his left elbow pushing the door open to his right elbow shutting the door—conservation of movement.

As he walked up to the front door of the small building, he could see the short, well-groomed, thick-haired, used-car-salesman face of Bert Ratso waiting behind the glass double doors. Good old Bert, Fred thought; at least he had enough sense to be nervous about some of the business he conducted.

"Fred, my friend. How are you?"

"Bert Ratso," Fred replied, wondering if Bert actually had any friends, or at least anyone who would admit to being his friend. "How are you?"

"Life is good, right, Fred?"

"Business is good then, Bert?"

"People always need information, and it seems even more so these days."

They shook hands, and Fred followed Bert up the stairs to his second floor, corner office. The door was open, and Fred waited for Bert to walk in first. As he walked in, Fred closed the door behind him and took out his wallet. He waited for Bert to sit down and then took the business card out of his wallet. He handed the card to Bert and then took five one thousand dollar bills out of his wallet, making certain to hold them up so that Bert, pretending not to notice, would see them.

"Rachel McCormack. McCormack is not exactly an unusual name, Fred."

"Yeah, but how many Rachels with that business address as a cross-reference will there be?"

Bert looked at Fred, a nervous smile passing across his face. "Of course, good point, Fred. Now this Amanda Carlini, she should be pretty easy."

"Look, Bert, we know each other. I need a comprehensive profile by this time tomorrow at the latest. Cross reference anything to do with relatives, especially a sister, maybe twenty-three to twenty-five years of age. But follow up on any level one family and associates. Any of them associated with the entertainment or modeling industries, do a quick shot. Or if any of them are attorneys. Need bank accounts on any level one family—and tell your contact it's not going to court or anywhere else, so I need account numbers too."

Fred placed the five thousand dollars on the desk in front of Bert and looked at him. Bert looked at the money, then up at Fred, and then took the money and shoved it quickly in his chest pocket Bert's way of saying this transaction was not going to be recorded anywhere. Fred smiled, put his wallet away, and extended his hand to Bert.

"Don't get up, Bert. You have work to do. Thank you, Bert. If you get it done before noon tomorrow, just put it in General Delivery."

Bert knew enough not to get up. He shook Fred's hand, and Fred walked out. Most people didn't know it, but many post offices still maintained a General Delivery area. And if someone dropped something there for you, it never went through all the normal post office processing as long as you picked it up right away. Mentioning the option to Bert was Fred's way of letting Bert know he expected it to be there by noon. The comprehensive might take him fifteen minutes to pull, the related short profiles five or ten each. With outlining and cross-referencing, Bert had a total of maybe four to six hours of work.

Fred walked slowly back down to his car, paying close attention for any sounds or movement in the building. As he stepped outside, he held the door for a moment, scanned the lot, and then proceeded to his car. He went over a mental checklist of what he had done that day and what was still left to do. Patience, Fred, he reminded himself. He would wait until after he picked up Bert's report and reviewed it to decide what his next step should be. Shrimp arrabbiata and some raspberry gelato sounded good. And then, hopefully, some good sleep.

***

9:30 p.m.

Mark watched as Amber ate the last few bites of cherry pie. At twenty-three, she had seen as much of the ugliness of the world as Mark. *Experienced it*, Mark thought, correcting himself. A world of difference between knowing about and feeling it first-hand. Although she had been clean for almost six months, Mark couldn't help but wonder whether she'd ever get completely clear. Born to two grafter parents who didn't know how to see anyone as anything other than a target for a scam, she had become one of their tools early on. More than once Mark had wondered if Amber wouldn't have been better off if they had sold her to someone right away.

"Amber, you still clean?"

"C'mon, Mark, cut me a little slack. If I was using again, you think I'd be able to remember details to give to you? 'Sides, you aren't asking me to testify or nothin', right?"

"Nope. I still have to be able to rely on the information, though. Stoned snitch is no good to me."

"Informant, sir," Amber said, a smile flashing across her face and disappearing quickly.

"Informant, sorry," Mark replied and smiled. Amber didn't have much to hold onto, and Mark understood that sometimes it did matter what you called it. After all, you didn't call a lobbyist a professional briber and white collar criminal. "So, tell me."

"Okay, just a minute. Little coffee."

"Of course."

103

"Now," Amber said, putting her coffee cup down. "I come out of this house where I got done with a client, and I'm just going to walk over to my place, done for the night. I'm walking down eighteenth, and I see this car stopped by one of the driveways. Nice car. Newer Lexus. Not parked really, like he was driving at the driveway, at an angle. Car backs out from there and drives like two houses down on the opposite side, pulls to the curb at the same kind of angle. Got my curiosity. Door opens and this white dude gets out. Dressed nice. Got that white and gray kind of hair. What you guys call...salt and...salt and pepper. Gets out, and he's like mumbling to himself. Couldn't make it out, but he wasn't happy. Definitely got my interest now."

"Could you see if anyone was with him?"

"No, no it wasn't anyone else in the car I could see. At some point though, he's sayin' something about Rachel. Said that name two or three times."

"Rachel. You're sure it was Rachel?"

"Oh, it was no mistaking it, least twice anyways. It was loud enough anybody out on the block could have heard. No, it wasn't anybody else out I saw."

"Jesus," Mark said, drawing in a breath, not ready to accept the possibility. "I need a cigarette. You want a cigarette?"

"You still smokin' them Indian cigarettes?"

"Yup. Only organic cancer for me," Mark joked and stood up. "You still enrolled in classes?"

"Show up every day, boss. Going to get that license."

Mark stepped up to the register and, handing the cashier his credit card, said, "Petey, how you doin'?"

"Tired, Mark. Just tired right now. You want to put a tip on that?"

104

"For Robin? Sure. Five bucks."

"You have a good night, Mark. Stay safe."

"Always do, Petey. Always do."

As they stepped out front, Mark took his keys out of his pants pocket and let the heavy weight of the metal disc at the end of the long set of chains fall, causing the keys to slightly jangle. He let the door close and stepped to his left. He grasped the car key between his index and middle fingers.

"You do always have something at the ready, don't you?"

"Amber, my dear, I do try to stay safe."

"What's that at the bottom?"

"A sort of paperweight, I guess. Got it from one of the runs a friend talked me into. A pound and a half of metal that can make a nice dent when swung correctly."

"Nice. No wonder you talk about peace like you do; you're ready for the opposite."

"Clever, Amber," Mark said and took his cigarettes out, offering the open pack to her. He took one out and lit hers first. "Now, you're sure that he was saying Rachel?"

"No doubt about that," Amber replied and inhaled deeply, her eyes closed for a moment, her head tilted up to the sky. "Couldn't make out much else, but said that name a couple—few times."

"Okay. Did you get a good look at him?"

"Not, like, up close. I didn't want any part of whatever he had goin' on. He was about five ten, slimmer than you, but not thin. Maybe your age or a few years older. Thin features. Had a nice, full length coat on...some kinda cloth, not leather or suede."

"Wool, maybe?"

"Yeah, dressy like that. What's going on? You think you know the dude?"

"You have learned much in your young years, Amber," Mark answered, pausing for a moment to take a deep inhale. People who grew up with lives like Amber learned to watch people, read people. The kind of skills many investigators had to go to schools like Reid and Associates to try to learn. "Look, I have to go, but if you're right, I may just pay for a semester of that massage school. You have to promise, though: once you get that license, all legit. No happy endings."

"Damn, boss. You do keep it real."

"Go home, Amber. Get some sleep."

"You too, old man."

Mark pretended a stern look, and they both smiled. He watched her walk across the street, the apartment she was renting not far from the small diner. As he walked around to the parking lot on the side, he stopped for a moment. He crushed out the cigarette he had been smoking and tossed the butt into the garbage can against the café wall. He immediately took out another, nervously considering the possibility that Tim was not out of town that weekend, and, more than that, was possibly at that party. It was a lot to consider, and there were certain facts that could be verified but not until the morning. He inhaled deeply and walked to his car. As he reached to put the key in the car door, he decided he would have to ask Rachel for Tim's personal cell. It would be a difficult conversation, but he would try not to bring the dark side of the possibilities immediately to the forefront.

As he was about to put the key in the door, he heard a car speeding around the corner behind him, tires squealing from a turn taken too sharply. He dropped to a crouching position and shifted to face the intersection. *Nice time to have your jacket in the car, shithead*, he yelled at himself.

"Hey, asshole! What you hiding from?"

You fucking asshole, he thought and stood up.

"Real subtle, Bob," Mark said and stepped toward the familiar SUV. "Surprised you didn't put that over the PA."

"I owed you that one."

"Maybe. But I'm guessing you're not here just to be a dick."

"Hey, you're the dick. I'm the flatfoot."

"Well, if you're gonna date yourself like that, the appropriate name would be gumshoe. But since I don't look like Sam Spade or Phillip Marlowe, and you definitely don't look like Detective Tom Polhaus, maybe we should fast forward."

"All right, wise-guy, thanks for the history recap. You know, you should think about pulling a Dashiel Hammett sometime soon. From what I've seen, it looks like there's a lot more money in writing the fiction than working the reality."

"Hmm. Save that thought for another discussion. How did you find me anyway?"

"The price you pay for carrying a cell phone."

"I'm guessing this is pretty important if you called on someone for the trace. And you're not sure how important; hence the display of nervous energy."

"You know, shylock," Bob said and motioned for Mark to step away from the vehicle. "I could have used someone like you in my unit back in the day."

Bob parked and got out.

"Thanks, Bob," Mark replied, knowing that was a compliment Bob would not give easily. "Not sure how well I'd do in a firefight."

"No one knows 'til they're in one. Let's walk a little."

"You're not going to try to hold my hand are you?"

"Shut up asshole."

They only walked a short distance from the restaurant when Bob stopped. He looked around. There was some foot traffic on Halsted but no one walking down Eighteenth. They could hear music and conversations coming from nearby apartments but none with people out on the front porch.

"I couldn't talk about this before. Even I don't know all the eyes and ears at the station. There's been a series of disappearances over the last thirteen months. Only connection with the victims is that they're all tied in to modeling somehow, and they've all been in some form of recovery."

"Recovery? You mean like AA?"

"Like that."

"Doesn't fit my client's sister."

"Nope, which might be good news, but no way to know."

"Why? What happened to the others? Were they all killed in the same way? What makes it appear serial?"

"I suspect they might have been. But we have not found a single body. It's one thing that helped us to keep it out of the papers. They've all just disappeared."

"Justino family showed up in any of the others?"

"Not that we can tell. But, there's the other part. One of my snitches over at the Inspector General's Office called earlier."

"Ain't that America?" Mark interjected.

"Yeah, we just hide our corruption better. Truth is, professional politicians' addiction to power and self-aggrandizement is no different anywhere. Wrap themselves in patriotism. Hell, as long as their kids don't have to go to war, they'll go to war for anything. They'll talk about God and country, as long as it's you they're telling to walk into a village and gun down women and children based on faulty intelligence, as long as it's you pulling the trigger or..."

Mark reached over and placed a hand on Bob's shoulder. Bob stopped speaking and breathed in deeply, closing his eyes for a moment. As he exhaled, his eyes opened.

"Okay...okay. Thanks, Mark. Oh, and you can take your other hand from behind your back with those keys dangling now." They looked at each other for a moment and then laughed lightly. There were times when Bob would go off on a rant that was quite emotional. Given his size and physique, it was not surprising that people worried what was going to happen next. Mark knew Bob knew how to control himself. They both knew Mark was not foolish enough to try to make the key defense work against Bob. "Thanks, Mark. I wonder sometimes if Liz being a nurse is what allows her to handle the emotional darkness the way you do."

"Cops marrying nurses is not a new thing. Although you're a Sox fan, and she's a Cubs fan; not sure how that works."

"Right. You know, you really should think about that though—having someone who can be there."

"Very good, sir. Take it under consideration, sir."

"Okay, okay, I read you. You're right, though. It is pretty messed up. Needing a snitch at the Mayor's Office of the Inspector General is pretty much an indictment on the reality of our democratic system.

"And that kind of analysis is why you got that Master's degree, right?"

"No, but it sure got me an offer I could refuse. Politics later, though. Apparently Michael himself was downtown talking to people about making arrangements for an exclusive event in a week. You know, the kind where everyone on duty acts as if those two blocks suddenly didn't exist."

"No patrols, no tactical, no anybody?"

"Ten-four. Not sure if there's a connection to your girl, but it's a hell of a coincidence."

"If you believe in those."

"Right. Look, Mark, you can't share this with your client yet. If she…"

"I know," Mark interjected. "Even if she says she won't talk about it, she will. So, where does this leave us?"

"Mostly in the same place, except we got a call tonight from an anxious mom about her daughter, who's a model. Which makes me worry that if it's our guy, something has pushed him over a bit. Makes me worry he's already decided what to do about your client's sister."

"Damn," Mark said. He knew Bob was right. "I'm guessing you'd say it's time to step it up and go harder, even on hunches."

"Hmmm, we do know each other…you think we're like Butch and Sundance? Or Laurel and Hardy?"

"Cute, Bob," Mark replied. "Maybe Simon and Simon?"

"You're the pretty one. All right, I have to be back at Grand Central in a half hour…got two witnesses on that g.d. scuffle coming in."

"Bob, when you going to tell the thugs they have to come in during office hours?"

"Soon as you tell your clients that twenty-four-hour availability costs more per hour."

"Fair enough. Take care of business. We'll talk soon."
"Ten-four."

They walked back to their vehicles and got in. Mark turned his car on but waited and watched as Bob pulled out onto Halsted. He was even less sure what to think about the possibility of Antoinette being alive. Did Tim fit any kind of profile? It was a lot to process, and he was tired. Part of him wanted to stay up and work on it. He knew that would not make for him being very useful tomorrow, and there was a bottle of Don Julio Anejo which needed a shot glass worth of draining. He shifted into drive and started the journey home.

CHAPTER FIVE

Thursday, June 23rd
9:20 a.m.

"I'm not sure I understand, Mark," Rachel said and sat down in the chair Andre had pushed toward her. She understood clearly the facts that Mark had told her, but her brain was resisting any of the implications brought by them. Better to let him fully explain. He would probably take them an entirely different path than her mind had leaped to. He would explain a different, more rational and reasonable explanation. Tim was bingeing, and he didn't want her to know.

"I'm sorry, Rachel. There's really no way to be less than blunt about this. Tim may have left for his family cabin on Friday morning, but he was back in the city before Sunday last weekend."

"That is blunt. How do you know? What makes you certain? He called me that Saturday, excited about a big musky."

"He called a couple times, Mark," Andre added. "Once before the musky call."

Rachel twisted around to look at Andre, still standing behind her. "I don't remember that, Andre."

"I only remember because you had said it was funny he called early in the weekend. You said he didn't usually call until Sunday, mostly when he was ready to head back."

"Makes sense. Do you remember anything about that first call, Rachel?"

"Trying to," Rachel answered and closed her eyes for a minute. "Wait, yes. Yes I do remember. He called just to check on me because he knew I was worried about Annie. Said he felt a little guilty when he got there, knowing we had an argument."

"It's funny too," Andre added, "Because Annie said there was something about Tim she didn't like, didn't trust."

"She did? When did she tell you that, Andre?" Rachel demanded, her volume quickly rising.

"I'm sorry, Rae. She asked me to keep quiet about it. There was some things she just felt she couldn't talk to you about. Pretty much what happens when you take over that role of looking out for her."

"He's right, Rachel. Some of that kind of thing between siblings is unavoidable. And, if I were Andre, I probably wouldn't have said anything either—put it off to Annie not liking Tim just because."

"I still don't understand the calls. Why would he lie about catching a fish?"

"People who lie, especially regularly or pathologically, will throw in details, additional information to make it seem more authentic, more real. I had a girlfriend one time. Told me a couple details about a party she attended, but, oops, the person she said she was talking to was across the table from me holding a full house, queens high. Not very clever people can be obvious to someone who's looking. They give themselves away by selectively answering your questions and providing detail that is unnecessary or irrelevant and, unfortunately for them, often verifiable."

"So, what did you do?"

"What did I do? Oh, you mean my girlfriend at the time. Generally, I try to be respectful even of people who are less than kind to me, but I couldn't resist. I showed our friend the text, and he gave her a call a few seconds later. He played dumb for a couple of minutes and then mentioned where he was."

"Ouch. That's cold."

"Yes, but it eliminated a lot of unnecessary conversation."

"I guess I'll try to stay on your good side. So I get what you're saying, but how does that work with Tim? He's always up there alone. That's part of what works for him."

"Everyone makes mistakes, Rachel. I'll be honest and tell you I came across the information by accident, but that's why I trust it a little more. You always have to be a little suspicious when a street source tells you just what you want to hear, but when they give up something you weren't looking for, you tend to believe it more. Tim was seen driving around the Pilsen neighborhood. Got out of the car a couple times. Snitch took down the plate because it was an unusual car in the neighborhood and a had a police friend run it."

"Wait a minute. You're telling me one of your street sources has cop friends that run plates for him?"

"Her, actually. But, yes."

"That's what I mean when I tell you sometimes 'bout it being too long since you've been down on the block, Rachel," Andre said. "Back in the day, that would be no surprise to you Street side gets much stranger than that."

"Down on the block? Down on the block. Andre, you playing old school for Mark's benefit."

"Well, you know, I'm guessing he only gets his street talk off of some show on HBO or Netflix, and that be two years old at best."

"Thanks, Rachel. Thanks Andre. Always good to get a reminder of age and..."

"So, you have no doubt? You don't think this girl got the plate wrong or anything?"

"Considered that until she described the car and Tim pretty well. I need his personal cell number before I say anything more."

"Mark, I don't know. I should ask…"

"Rae," Andre said firmly and stepped up to her, placing a hand on her shoulder. "This is about Annie—you and Annie. Tim's not first consideration here."

"He's right, Rachel. This time it's about taking care of Annie. If I'm wrong, I'll apologize and buy you two a weekend away, but if I'm right? Well, let's just say it changes everything."

"But…"

"Rachel, you're my client. Tim's not. You're not the first client I've had to talk to this way; you probably won't be the last. It's important, and I can't explain until I know for sure. It could just be Tim's steppin' out on you. This is my job, to find out. Let me do my job."

Mark hesitated for a moment, drawing a deep breath and listening to Rachel. He was glad Andre was there with her. He would have to talk to Andre later. Whether or not Andre made contact with anyone who had information held less importance at the moment. Following this up came first.

He took another deep inhale. He hated making the call, but he didn't want to waste any time. If Amber was right, something was very wrong with Tim, and that could mean a lot of different things. He would have to call in a favor from a friend at Verizon, but as he had learned many years ago, despite what many people said, you do what you can for people because it's the right thing to do. Someday you might need their help, and hopefully they'll remember.

"So, what now? What do I do?" she asked and leaned forward, elbows on her knees, hands on her chin. "What the hell is going on, Mark?"

"Yeah," Mark said. He got up and stepped over to her. "For now, you have to try to trust me and find somewhere to be. Have Andre take you somewhere, maybe visit some friends in the old neighborhood. Tim might not call, but in case he does..."

"Right. Great."

He placed his hands on her shoulders and squeezed. Her instinct was to shrug them off. He had just given her disturbing information about someone she loved. What the hell did he think he was doing trying to comfort her? His hands very gently pushed down, a warmness spreading from them. Her instinct was put on hold, and she sat back in the chair, closing her eyes tightly and letting the wetness gathering in the corner of her eyes flow freely. She inhaled deeply and the darkness behind her eyes seem to fold in on itself, doubling - it was all going to get much more difficult.

***

11:15 a.m.

Fred sat in his car in the post office parking lot and read quickly through the report. Bert had highlighted all the areas he thought applied to what he had been told. Amanda Carlini was living on one of the Aeolian Islands, which was not surprising. Fred noted that and scanned her report to ensure he had bank account information—everything overseas was much easier. At the back was her picture.

She was gorgeous. The wide smile and squinting left eye highlighted the influence of her father. It made him think of a conversation with Sam, a conversation he was surprised got lost in his memory until now. Or, he thought, that part of his mind had suppressed.

"So, Fred," Sam Carlini had said, standing on the deck of his ranch home in Riverdale. "I almost envy you. You know, the old ways…you almost had to drink just to stay sane. I mean you'll still be doing the same job essentially, but without all the mess."

"I'm not sure I follow you, Sam. I mean about the drinking."

"The blood, the fights, the bodies. It's not pleasant work. After a while, most guys get to drinking and just keep drinking—all the time."

"How'd they get anything done?"

"Functional is the word that's used, Fred. When I was in the Army, we had a Sergeant, drank a half pint every morning with his coffee. He'd had some rough experiences in Korea. Ninety-five percent of the time, he did his job just fine; the other five percent we all covered for him."

"Shit, Sam, I hope he wasn't a sniper or nothin'."

"Motor pool, Fred. Motor pool. But my point is, his drinking started when he was in the jungle, killing people and being a target. You have an advantage with this new approach. You make these people have "accidents." You don't have to be there, see a lot of it. And except when they want you to send a message to the other families so they know who offed the person, no immediate heat comes your way."

"Yeah, Sam, I guess that's true."

"This little glass," Sam had said, raising the lowball filled with his favorite sipping whiskey and ice, "Has helped many a man numb his emotions and avoid nightmares."

"Avoid nightmares," Fred said aloud, bringing himself back to the moment. Of course he had that nightmare. Everything was coming back to him now, without the whiskey. All those assignments...all those assignments were people, and that was something Fred had not thought about in a very long time.

"All for a reason," Fred said, remembering what he had heard at several meetings. He looked back at the envelope and pulled out another report. "Now, maybe I can figure this out."

Antoinette McCormack, age twenty-six, was employed by at least one modeling agency, and since the reports now included pictures when available, Fred was certain of the identity of the mystery woman who was part of his rude awakening. Seeing Tim Vanderschmidt's name among Rachel's level one associates made Fred stop reading.

"Jesus fu...sorry, sorry," Fred said and put the report down on the passenger seat for a minute. What Sam Carlini had said about unexplainable or irrational incidents came immediately to mind. What were the odds that Tim was his sponsor and a level one associate of Rachel McCormack's? What sense would it possibly make that Tim were somehow involved? What would Tim have to do with any of it?

Fred reached inside the large envelope and pulled out the profile report on Tim. He read through it quickly and stopped as soon as he saw that Tim had been employed by Morgan and Bernstein, P.C. Like many law firms, they chose the Professional Corporation designation to ensure that no one but other attorneys could work for the firm. Like most law firms employed by the Justino family, they had a wide reach and a low profile.

Now, Fred knew, there was really only one question left. And it was a question he would have to ask Don Justino himself. Was Tim now part of the family again? If not, the course of action was much more clear and direct. Tim was the only connecting tissue in all of it. And one thing Fred knew was that connective tissue, no matter how slight or seeming to hover at the edges, was where the explanation lay. It was a weird thought, but somehow his sponsor either was responsible for this mess or knew who was. Either way, Fred thought, there was only one possible outcome, and it didn't involve twelve fucking steps.

* * *

1:10 p.m.

Tim looked at the bottle of gin. It was more than a bottle of gin; it was a sort of trophy. For fifteen years now, no matter what happened on that one weekend a month, the bottle of Tanqueray on his fireplace mantle remained unopened, intact. As his right hand moved, striking the wheel of the lighter, Tim flinched and dropped it.

"What the hell?"

Tim looked around. He was home alone, but that made him feel even more conscious of the fact he had almost lit a cigarette in the house. He didn't smoke in the house, he didn't smoke in the car, and didn't remember taking the pack out of the car, much less the cigarette out of the pack. It was like two weeks ago in the kitchen. He was cutting up limes to squeeze over the swordfish steaks he had been preparing for himself and Rachel and looked down to see he had cut them thin, as if he were going to be dropping them into a glass with some gin and tonic. Luckily, Rachel had come over exhausted that night and had been stretched out on the sofa.

He looked back over at the bottle on the mantle. Was the paper that ran over the top of the bottle broken? Had someone opened the bottle? Was someone else there with him? Why was there only one light, the bathroom light? And was that the sound of water running?

Tim stepped over to the antique vanity that he used as a desk. It was a simple piece of hand-carved furniture. Elegant, but simple, with one small center drawer. One of the interesting features to Tim was that the center of the top was an inset of naugahyde. The use of naugahyde had become popular in the early 1930s, but it was not always typically used in conjunction with high-end furniture. The edges of the top were wood, and the naugahyde center was perfect for his computer; it withstood the placement of coffee or other cups without damage. On the back was a tall mirror, as wide as the whole desk. It was a separate piece held on by screws, but Tim never removed it. His father had never removed it. It was the only piece of furniture he had brought down from the cabin.

"Why didn't you call it in, Timothy? Why?"

Although he was looking into the mirror, his stare was blank. His mind was back in Wisconsin, thirty-five years ago. His father had been standing behind him. It had been late fall, and he had been sitting at the vanity on the small wooden chair his father almost worshipped. It was a chair that his mother had brought home when they had closed down the old church, the church that his father insisted was more than God would ever have asked for. After all, his father had shouted, were his sermons going to be any more inspired by the idolatrous new building, furniture, and luxuries?

"Sit there, Timothy," his father had said. "Sit there and look in that mirror, young man. Look into your eyes, your soul. Your black, empty soul. Your vain, pleasure-obsessed soul."

"Da…father…I…," he had started to respond before feeling the snapping crack of his father's knuckles on the back of his head. "It wasn't my fault."

"Of course not. That's what all sinners say. You're weak. You're weak, and you need to be punished."

Tim had heard the snapping sound of his father's belt pulled quickly out of belt loops. He closed his eyes, as he had learned to do. He had closed his eyes and prayed for forgiveness and delivery as he felt the first smack of the belt across his back. When it stopped—he had not known how long it had gone on—he opened his eyes and looked into that mirror.

"Sinners, all of them," Tim said, still staring into the mirror. He was not himself, but he was back in the present. He was back to punish. It was Fred's time. Fred, who after working for the worst of people, wanted sympathy and mercy because he drank too much. Of course he drank too much. Of course he did not have control of his drinking. He did not have control of his life. Because he did not give control of his life over to God.

"Why didn't you call it in? Timothy!"

Tim heard his father yell. His father knew why he didn't call it in. He was weak. He was drunk. He served the Lord's purpose, removing temptation from the young harlot, helping Rachel's sister find her salvation without leading a continued, cursed life, without traveling down a path from which there might be no hope of turning back, of finding mercy.

He didn't call it in. He didn't call the police and have Fred caught for the kind of crime he had committed over and over again: taking the lives of others, not because he was called upon by a higher power but because of the direction of people who knew only the rewards of this material place. Going to that party without even thinking about Annie being there was his first mistake; he had corrected that before she had a chance to tell Rachel anything. He didn't call it in, but it was not too late to correct that mistake as well.

He reached into his shirt pocket and took out another cigarette, looking over at the bathroom door hanging half open. Why did it sound as if water were running? He bent down, picked up the lighter, and lit his cigarette.

Tim walked over to the small bureau by the bathroom hallway and opened the bottom drawer. He reached in, his eyes closed, his hand finding the Beretta .22 resting on top of, instead of between, two neatly folded hand towels. Why was it out of place?

He stepped into the bathroom and saw the stiletto heels thrown at the base of the shower first. He stepped quickly to turn the water off that was flowing in the tub. For a moment, he was disturbed because he couldn't remember anything about the young woman. He saw that the bath water was clear. There was no longer any blood draining from her body.

"You go to a better place," he said.

He didn't have time to address the matter of her body at the moment. A flash of memory burst into his mind. The first time it had happened.

He had first started going to the family cabin with the intention of avoiding the temptations of the city. Hike, canoe, even chop wood. He would exorcise his demons by exhausting his body. It had worked for six months. Then, a little over a year ago, after losing a copyright infringement case, he had stumbled upon his father's hidden liquor cabinet. He couldn't remember how he had gotten to Chicago or who the dead woman in his condo was, but he knew he had to do something quickly. That first time, it had been messy and nervous work.

"Kingston was the only real accident," he said, the sound of his own voice bringing him back to the moment. "I think I know what to do with you, young lady."

He would take care of Fred and then take this body over to Fred's house. This time, he would call the police right away. It would work.

He looked down at the gun in his hand and held it for a moment, his eyes closed. He gripped it tightly and smiled.

"I'll make it right, father. I have seen the error, and I will make it right."

***

2:30 p.m.

"Thanks for coming on short notice, Andre," Mark said and waited for Andre to sit down before he sat. "Mocha with an extra shot."

"Thanks, Mark," Andre replied and took a sip of the drink.

"I'm not really a Starbucks kind of guy, but they do make great dessert coffees."

"Dessert coffees?"

"Just what I call the mochas and fraps and stuff. They're not like a regular cup of coffee; they're more like a treat."

"Right, clever. So, I only made a few phone calls, but there are two people who were at the party. One of them remembers seeing Annie. They both said they'd talk to you."

"Good work, Andre. Now you get to think less of me," Mark said, a smile flashing quickly across his face and then disappearing. He saw the puzzled look on Andre's face and took a sip of his coffee. "Sorry, bad sense of humor. Talking to them is taking a back seat for the moment. If Tim was in town that weekend and has been lying to Rachel about it, there's a good reason. It could be something as simple as he's cheating on her, but I want to know before we spend time on anything else."

"You're worried something bad happened to Annie," Andre said, sat back in his chair, and sipped his drink. "And Tim might have something to do with it?"

"No wonder Rachel trusts you so much. I don't really have much to explain it though, except that most of the time, people know the person who does bad things to them."

"I do know that, for sure," Andre replied. "People don't like to hear it, but family's often the first people you need to look at."

"Unfortunately, true. Don't mean to be rude, but I just wanted to talk to you in person, even if it has to be rushed. I want you to stay with Rachel as much as you can."

"Well, that's not a problem. Unless Tim shows up sudden-like, Rae always likes my company."

"Not alone much?"

"Oh, she likes her alone time as much as anyone else—plays her piano, reads a bit. We all need to have our down time...you know, take care of yourself without thinking or worrying on nobody else. Me, I like to shop. What about you, Mark. How do you decompress?"

Mark looked at Andre for a moment, caught completely off guard. For his mother, Bob, and anyone else he knew, he had an answer at the ready for why he didn't need anyone in his life or make room for the kind of time Andre was talking about.

"Fishing," Mark replied.

"Not one I could ever understand, but I know a few people who can forget the world that way."

"All right. I need to go get these things done," Mark said, stood up and grabbed his coffee. "I'll text when I have some idea of where this is going."

"Okay, Mark. I'm going to see if I can find something for Rae to nibble on—she's horrible about not eating when she's upset. Maybe I'll stop and get her one of her favorite teas too—Mariano's is the only place I know that sells it, organic and all that."

"Now that," Mark said, starting walking toward the door, "Does not surprise me. I know a few women like that, and the others seem to go the opposite direction."

"Opposite direction for me—eat a whole pizza by myself when I'm bluesy. You be careful out there."

"I am. Thanks, Andre."

***

3:20 p.m.

"Come on up, Andre" Rachel said, pressing the button. She left the door slightly open, walked over to the sofa, and sat back down. The album was open to Annie's high school graduation. The second year after their father's death. He would have been so proud of his baby girl.

"Rae, I got your favorite cinnamon roll and tea. Should I bring them in there?"

"Sure, Andre," Rachel replied and set the book down on the coffee table. "Not worried about crumbs in the carpet right now."

"That's a good thing, Rae," Andre said.

"Not sure what you mean, Andre," Rachel said as Andre walked into the room. He had put the cinnamon roll on a plate, grabbed a napkin, and helped himself to one of the cold coffees in the refrigerator. "Take a seat and tell me."

"Oh, you know, just let little things go cuz it's a lot goin' on right now."

"You think I've gotten a bit uptight?"

"Wow, now I wasn't saying all that. What makes...oh, you got the pictures out."

"Yup. Annie's graduation. We went down to the lake afterwards. Don't know what got into her, but she ran into the lake, cap and gown still on. I followed her. Ruined a six thousand dollar Armani. Didn't hesitate. Not one second."

"That's my Rae-Rae," Andre said, smiling and laughing. "You did some crazy stuff."

"I did, didn't I?" Rachel asked, feeling the sadness creep in, the melancholy. No one but Andre and her father ever called her their Rae-Rae. And she never felt like stopping Andre from using it. He knew their father, and knew the bond she had with him. "When did I stop?"

"C'mere, Rae," Andre said, holding open his arms, "I know that tone."

"No wonder daddy liked you."

"Now, just because you could afford to pay for that Armani didn't make it a good decision. But I know Annie appreciated it when you were a little...less serious."

"You've never really said anything."

"Oh, I have. Just been too subtle. You know, never had any real worries like this. When she's back, maybe you two should take a weekend, go to New Mexico or something."

"I do love the desert."

"When was the last time you went, Rae? When was the last time you got up and went down to play at House of Blues? I mean, I'm not trying to be hard, but Annie misses having an older sister, someone who's more friend than mother."

"You think that's why she doesn't like Tim?"

"I think it started before Tim, but yes, he's wired pretty tight."

"Wired pretty tight," Rachel repeated and closed her eyes for a moment. She swallowed hard. She was not afraid to cry in front of Andre; they had both cried together before. But there was something about what he said, about Tim being wired pretty tight. There was something at the edge of her mind that wasn't coming. Maybe it wasn't important, but right now she wasn't sure what was or wasn't important.

"What is it, Rae?"

"I don't know," she answered and reached over for the plate with the cinnamon roll. "Probably nothing. Thank you for this, and the tea."

"Just hope you remember next time Lucius gets all drama on me."

"Maybe there's something for you to think about?"

"Maybe," Andre replied, holding a straight face as long as he could before laughing.

"So tell me a little more about it. Remind me, Andre."

Andre knew what she meant, and she listened as he reminisced about times they had shared and stories he had been told by her and Annie. Some went back to the old neighborhood, and some went to trips to Hawaii and other places. He talked about the two trips the three of them had made to New Mexico and grabbed the book to search for the pictures of her and Annie acting silly at Carlsbad Caverns as the bats were coming out.

"You know, Andre, I couldn't have a better brother."

"Thanks, Rae. I love you too. But much as you couldn't exactly call me a U2 fan, it's a thing about lyrics for me. You may not know this one, but the song itself was popular. The line is "the right to appear ridiculous is something I hold dear." It's something in that, Rae."

"Sometimes I wonder how you understand so much, Andre. Now I need you to understand, I need a little time to myself. Maybe play a little."

"Okay, long as you promise me the ash tray stays out on the balcony. Took me a week to get that smell out last time you were playing and drinking."

"I promise. Although I probably won't be drinking hard. Not right now. When Annie gets back..."

"Margarita and pizza on the veranda," Andre said as he started walking toward the door, adding a British accent on the last three words.

"Yes, of course, on the veranda," Rachel replied and gave him a strong hug before he stepped out.

***

Her fingers slowed down on the keyboard as the memory started to form. It had been a warm August day, and they finished a late breakfast and decided to take a walk along the lakefront. The breeze was light, but it was enough to keep the humidity at bay. Tim had said something about Annie, about how her behavior was leading her down a path away from God. Spending so much time with people who live away from the Word.

"Don't get me wrong, Tim. I think I'm pretty good with God, but don't go throwin' the Bible at me. Frankly, I wonder why so many people who call themselves Christian go around quoting Old Testament when they find people to hate."

"What? What do you mean, Rachel?"

"C'mon, Tim. To me, *Christian* means follower of Christ. You know, New Testament."

"I've seen a lot of people come to the program who make their lives better because they turn it over."

"She's not an addict that I know of Tim. Just because she's around it, doesn't mean she's in it."

"How long before she goes down that road?

"I didn't. And Annie saw some of the same people fall apart."

"I'm just worried, that's all."

"And I love you for it, Tim," she had said and kissed him on the cheek. "She's a little reckless, but who's not at that age?"

"But the people she associates with, some of them live...against all the teachings."

"Please, Tim. What teachings? Pretty sure Jesus was all about calling out the hypocrites and striking down all the details—you know, the simpler commandments that make sense. Is Andre destined to be rejected because of who he loves? He lives a more Christian life than most people I knew at the Baptist church growing up."

"I'm sorry, Rachel," Tim had said and seemed to drop the sort of angry tone his words carried at first. "I didn't mean it like that. Andre worries me sometimes because the musicians he associates with can speak violently and rudely in their songs, but I don't worry about who he dates."

"That's why he doesn't hang out with most of them outside the shows. Look, Tim, I know you mean well. But, there's some things you have to remember you don't understand well—growing up white in the suburbs can give you a whole different perspective, perhaps even a little less tolerance if your parents aren't educating you that at home."

"My parents were..."

"Wow, big guy. Not saying anything about your parents. But racism, and most of the other -isms, start at home. By the time kids get into school, they're already tuning out anything that goes against that home schooling we all get."

"Okay, sorry. Maybe we could change the subject?"

"That sounds good to me. Too nice of a day to argue about nothing."

"About nothing," Rachel repeated, bringing herself out of the memory. She looked down to see her fingers were bouncing quickly across the keys, almost banging them. The memory had started at the slowing of a Mary Lane song, a song she thought about whenever she was feeling grateful for friends like Andre. She was now belting out angry Bonnie Lee.

"Not sure what's happening, but I wonder if it was nothing," she said and closed the lid on the keys. She wanted a cigarette. She grabbed the tea off the table and walked to the balcony. What had Tim been doing?

***

6:40 p.m.

Fred pulled slowly into the alley of the old warehouse district in the Pilsen neighborhood. He still thought the only reason Don Justino liked to meet in these places was because he had nostalgia for the old days. Fred couldn't argue there was a security angle in meeting at places that didn't go back to you, places that weren't your regular haunts and were without witnesses, but the old warehouses seemed a stretch. His eyes

130

darted back and forth, looking for a door ajar, a window opened slightly, or any other sign of someone watching his approach. He knew there would be eyes on him once he got to the back of the building, but anyone watching sooner might indicate whether or not his suspicions were unfounded. Although Fred knew he was on the good side of Don Justino, he also knew that certain matters with the family had a traditional way they were addressed. Fred knew the Don could be smiling and talking with him and order his replacement to retire him five minutes later. Without a direct statement, there could be no certainty. If nothing else, Don Justino would not look him in the eye and lie to him.

As Fred pulled into the small lot behind the warehouse, a door opened quickly, and three men came out. Two walked out to the alley, and one came over to his door. Fred smiled. Good soldiers. He opened the door and got out with his hands interlaced on top of his head.

"Evening. Vito, right?" Fred said, a slight smile on his face as he felt the man's hands pressing and rubbing over his body. "Hey, Vito, don't be squeamish. You have to check the crotch, too. Never know where someone could stash a twenty-two or something."

"Right."

"I'm clean. Can we go now?"

"Vito," a voice yelled from the door, "If he's clean, let him come in. He's a friend."

Fred look over to the door. Whoever it was, he was not stepping out into the light, not taking the chance there might be cameras rolling somewhere. Wires could be good but not without other identification, and no one here was going to be mentioning names once they got inside. Vito would be a known commodity.

Fred stepped into the darkened warehouse and stepped behind the man who was already walking toward the small office with a light on. Whoever he was, he was obviously in charge of the crew here to protect the Don. He didn't recognize the voice, and the slow, deliberate steps were not those of people he recognized as being close to the Don.

"Fred," the man called over his shoulder as they got close to the office. "You know how this works. You have ten minutes of his time. Then, we leave. No disrespect. I know you know this, but don't waste time. Ten minutes, and you're on your way back to your car."

The man stopped at the door, reached for the handle, and turned to look at Fred. Fred did not recognize him at all. He was young though, maybe thirty-five or forty at the most. Michael DiNino, Fred thought. If Don Justino was letting him see who he was, that meant DiNino was soon to move up. Fred smiled and nodded as the door opened.

***

"Time for the truth, Tim," Fred said as he pulled out of the alley.

Tim had not been brought back into the family, and in the last week he had drawn attention to himself. He was asking questions of people he should know would talk. Maybe at some point he was all about the twelve steps, all about giving it over. It looked like that was only a part of a cover now, part of something he held out to people. His talk about confessing to move forward, just talk. It didn't make any sense at all, but in his gut, Fred knew Tim was responsible for this past week. He would explain, and he would pay a price.

Fred pulled the car over to the curb, put it in park, and took out his cell. He waited a moment, breathing in deeply, and exhaling slowly. He looked around quickly. There was foot traffic, but nothing suspicious. He looked up Tim and pressed call to dial.

"Tim. Yeah, it's me, Fred. Yeah, well, kinda. Need to talk to somebody. Really feeling the need for a drink. You can? Eleven o'clock...Really? No, no it's okay. Good. Sure. Melrose, right off North Avenue. Yeah. Okay, thanks Tim, thanks. Means a lot to me."

You'll never know how much, Fred thought. He pulled away from the curb and drove slowly. Tim wanted to meet at eleven, something about finishing up some work. It would give Fred time to go back to his house and then only forty-five minutes to get down to Melrose. It was good. He could get there and get set up. Tim lived in a world where being there on time made you look good. And, Fred thought, looking good seemed to be more of what Tim was about.

"See you soon, Tim," Fred said and slid the cell phone back in his jacket pocket. Tonight he would have all his answers.

***

8:10pm

"What are you doing, Mark?" Rachel asked. Mark had said that he had guns at the office, but she had never seen him take one out before. He had talked about resolving situations without them, how they were often a liability, not an asset. She watched as he opened the small cherry wood case he took out from the bottom drawer of the large, locking file cabinet.

"I thought you really didn't have much use for guns?"

"Rachel," Mark said and turned to look at her. "Being an idealist does not directly translate to being an idiot. Much as I don't like it, sometimes unreasonable people make it impossible to avoid   anything other than their inevitable conclusion. This isn't a movie, and I'm not some retired ninja assassin making everything okay without using guns. What I said almost always holds true. *Almost* always. Guns are, at best, a sometimes-necessary tool because people are not always reasonable or rational. When Bob Tyse tells me not to take any chances, I listen."

Rachel watched as Mark took the gun out of the case. It was a dull silver color with wooden grips. He took a magazine out of the box and slid it into the handle of the gun, slapping it tightly in, and then pulled the slide back. With the thumb of his hand holding the grip, he flipped up something. Probably a safety, she thought. Rachel had never had any guns, but between people she knew and every other movie painting them as an integral part of life, probably everyone knew some of the basics. What was it Roger Moore had said? He never regretted playing the part of James Bond; he only regretted that we live in a time when all our heroes are seen with a gun in their hand.

Mark took a small holster out of the box and clipped it to his belt on the right side. He slipped the gun into the holster as if it were an often-practiced motion.

"Mark," Rachel said, stood up, and walked over to him. "I...I want you to know, I..."

"Rachel," Mark interjected, reached out, and took her left hand in his hands, "I know you're grateful. You're also very hurt, sad, and confused. Your world fell out from under you quick. Keep it simple. You're my client, and I think you're a good person. I got your back, but just keep your head down until you get through this."

Rachel looked at him, fighting back both tears and anger. He was right, and he had realized it before she did. In another second, she would have reached out to hold him and kiss him, to try to believe it could all go away simply, that someone could be the person to make this all somehow less difficult. Part of her was angry at him for seeing that, but it was that same part that was holding the tears back, that strength that her daddy always admired.

"I have to go. Remember, it takes as much strength to allow the tears as to hold them back." Mark said and turned to the big window of the storefront office. Headlights splashed across the office as a car pulled into the parking lot. He released her hands, walked over to the other side of the office, and took her coat off the rack. "That will be Andre. He's going to take you home."

He held the black wool coat out for her. Rachel fought back the temptation to call him a presumptuous son of a bitch. He was right. She slipped the coat on and closed her eyes for a moment, letting out a deep, heavy sigh. She turned as the outer office door opened. Andre walked in, wearing his black leather jacket, black cargo pants, and a fedora cocked slightly forward. She couldn't help but wonder if Mark had asked him to dress the street tough part. Andre would take her home, and she could feel safe to let it all out. Andre would hold her and stay with her until she allowed herself to collapse into sleep.

"Thank you, Mark. Be careful."

"I will," Mark said and stepped over to open the inner office door. "Andre, how are you?"

"I'm all right, Mark. You ready to go, Rae?"

"I'm tired, Andre."

"You should be, Rae. It's a lot. C'mon," Andre said and stepped over to her, wrapping his arms around her and squeezing her tightly. She returned the hug with what little strength she had left, allowing her body to rest against his. She stepped back and turned to look at Mark.

"I'll be all right."

Rachel nodded and stepped out of the office with Andre. Mark hadn't told her much about where he was going, but she knew it was not going to be safe. As Andre held the door for her, she stepped out into the cool night air and said a silent prayer. She looked back one last time and saw Mark put an extra magazine in his coat pocket. As she got into Andre's car, she hoped that Mark would not find himself in a place where he needed that.

***

8:40 p.m.

"Yeah, the whole hundred thousand. No, I'll wait on the line for a confirmation number on the transfer...Yeah, I'll wait."

Fred looked around his kitchen, his eyes resting on the Keurig. Don Justino and most of his close people loved their espresso. Fred was not much of a fan. At the moment, he wanted a good, slow sip of the whiskey he had been drinking that night. It seemed appropriate, but it seemed even more appropriate to be perfectly sober for his sponsor.

"Mr. Batiste," the voice on the other end of the line said. "Are you still there?"

"Yeah, yeah, I'm still here. The transfer went through?"

"Yes, sir. Fifty thousand dollars into both of the accounts you specified. You realize, sir, that this empties your account? Did you want it to remain open?"

"No, no thank you."

"Very good, sir. You have a good evening."

"Yeah, you too," Fred replied and hit the disconnect button on his phone. He got up and walked to the bathroom. He paused for a minute and looked in the mirror. His eyes were looking old again but not quite the same as that morning. When he had gotten home, he looked at his personal photographs and realized he took Sam Carlini's advice to heart more than he realized. He overpaid for the nest tables. He sent a vacation trip to the sister of his assignment in France. He always tried to do something for the family of the people who were his assignments. He never felt bad about what he did to the people themselves. They were all involved in double-crossing or taking action against someone in the family; they deserved what happened to them. Their families didn't.

Whether or not Rachel McCormack needed the money didn't really matter. It was the only thing he could do for her. It was the same for Sam's daughter Amanda. Maybe fifty thousand wouldn't make a big change in her life. One thing he learned a long time ago, no matter how careful he was tonight, any number of circumstances could dictate he didn't return from his confrontation with Tim. So, he did what he could see to do.

He breathed a heavy sigh and checked the .380 one last time. He didn't know if he'd need it, and if he was right, he hoped he could bring a more personal touch to end Tim's life. But bringing only a knife to a gun fight was foolish. Overconfidence was not going to be what Fred wanted to be remembered for. He looked at his watch. It was time.

***

9:20 p.m.

Mark pulled up to the curb. He could see Tim's condo and the exit from the underground parking garage. It came out pretty much in the middle of Sheridan, so Mark was fairly confident he could stay with him no matter which direction he took. His friend at Verizon had been able to verify where Time had made the call about the musky and confirmed Tim was indeed in Chicago and on the near South Side that night. And he had verified for Mark that the cell was at Tim's condo.

Mark knew there was no way of knowing if or when Tim might leave his condo, but he also knew that Rachel had tried to hide her concern that she hadn't heard from Tim in the last couple days. Human behavior: the study most people did not attribute to private detectives, but one that was very important if you were going to be good. Tim dropping out of sight at this moment in Rachel's life was a clear signal that all was far from well. At the very least, he knew something about what happened. Bob's team had been able to go back through some history and put Tim as working for Morgan and Bernstein, P.C., a firm well known for their work on behalf of the Justino family.

Mark sat back, checking his mirrors and his phone. The phone was charged. As he set it down in the cup holder between the bucket seats, headlights could be seen starting up from the underground parking. There was no mistaking Tim's Lexus. *Good*, Mark thought, *I hate surveillance.*

He waited until a car got between him and the northbound Lexus and pulled out, not turning his headlights on until he was behind the car between him and Tim. It had cost him almost three hundred dollars to get the daytime running lights switched over to manual control, but it had proven to be worth it on more than one occasion. If your headlights came on as soon as your subject's did, they often took notice of your vehicle.

Mark felt his phone vibrate in his chest pocket and was tempted to ignore it. Following someone was not his strong suit, and this time it was really important. But if it was the boys or their mom calling, it could be just as important. She wouldn't call unless it was an emergency. When they were with her, it was up to him to call if he wanted to know how and what they were doing. His oldest, just turned seven, had even told him mommy said not to call daddy unless someone was hurt because daddy was probably working.

He took the phone out and looked. He was relieved it was not his ex calling; the boys were good. Bob Tyse calling was definitely important, though. He looked to make sure Tim was getting onto the ramp for the Eisenhower and then veered onto the ramp. He waited a moment, merging into traffic and allowing another car to get between and Tim and him. Fortunately, Tim seemed to be as methodical and precise in his driving as he was in most of his life. He tapped his turn signal and moved over into Tim's lane, three cars now between them. He took a cigarette from his chest pocket, lit it, and then reached for the phone. He picked it up and, without looking, pressed his thumbprint on the phone and then tapped on the phone icon, the call back feature taking over. It only rang once.

"Don't tell me you're driving, smoking, and talking to me at the same time, Mark."

"Okay, I won't tell you."

"And, the reason you don't have Bluetooth yet is because…"

"I have an earpiece. It's just…"

"Still in the box in your office drawer. All right, where you at, Mark?"

"Westbound on the Eisenhower. Apparently, Tim has some business in the burbs."

"Could be very serious business too, Mark. Michelsen earned her detective creds today. Tim used to be with Morgan and Bernstein. You keep me posted; I have a feeling I might be an off duty officer who just happened to be in your vicinity."

"Ten-four. Got some traffic coming up. Don't want to lose him."

"Throw me on the passenger seat; I'll wait. Got one more thing."

Mark tossed the phone on the passenger seat and flipped on his right turn signal quickly. Traffic was slowing, and a truck had started moving into his lane. He knew as they got close to the Harlem exit that being in the left lane did not mean you would be proceeding quickly. Visual contact was important in these circumstances. When you had two or three investigators on the road, you didn't have to be as worried about it. He could see Tim, and the semi was slowing traffic behind it. Mark's lane started moving past the left lane, and he tapped his turn signal again, this time pulling in just in front of the truck. He picked the phone back up. "Okay, boss, what's one more thing?"

"Two really. Text me Tim's number. I might could get my own system up to know where he's at."

"And..."

"And...something Sal Gianconno said is still running through my head, but I can't put it together yet. He said Tim was down there asking about that party, but he said there was also someone else asking, someone very few people knew."

140

"And he stopped there, I'll bet."

"Sal knows how to play it."

"Okay. Text it right after we get off the phone. Maybe I'll see you later."

"As you like to say, pro'ly."

Mark hit disconnect and then switched over to the text screen, his eyes darting back and forth from the road to the screen. Once the text had been sent, he tossed the phone on the passenger seat and ashed his cigarette out the slightly-open window. He took a deep inhale, wondering what Sal could have meant. If Bob wasn't sure, he knew it was not likely he'd have a good guess.

He focused his attention back on Tim and noticed his right turn signal was on. Mark was able to move two lanes over quickly and hoped Tim was headed to the split for 290. Traffic would be slightly less congested, and people tended to be going either seventy-five plus or staying just over sixty. Tim was staying with the just over sixty crowd. Careful, defensive driver. Mark knew that meant he needed to stay as generic a driver as anyone else on the road. He reached over and pushed the stereo button, hoping a little Rik Emmett would provide a pleasantly mild distraction so his nerves didn't get the best of him.

***

10:20 p.m.

Of course he wouldn't think twice about it, Tim thought. Fred was a professional killer to be afraid of if you were up against him, but he was not paid to think outside the logistics of an assignment. To Fred, Tim thought and smiled, Tim was his sponsor, someone who was there to help him through all the trials. Given the nature of his employment,

Tim was surprised Fred hadn't been in worse shape sooner. But then, Fred probably didn't consider much beyond the tactical aspects of his chosen profession.

The parking lot for the restaurant they had first gone to when Fred asked Tim to be his sponsor was under construction. The restaurant was still open, but the best parking was down the alley, almost a block away. With a couple of the adjacent streets under construction, Tim was confident there would be little, if any, foot traffic at this time on a Thursday night.

Tim reached over, popping open the glove box. The pack of cigarettes tumbled out and fell, open, onto the passenger seat. The pack was empty. Tim reached over and grabbed it, crushing it as he whispered a chorus of obscenities. He looked to the back seat quickly. The empty bottle of gin sat there alone. He started the chant again, certain he had bought another pack and set it beside the bottle before he got on the road.

He looked at the clock on his dash. He still had time. He pulled into the gas station on the corner, ran in quickly, and stepped out. He opened the packet, took one out, and lit it. Should he call Rachel, perhaps? Try to calm her nerves? Surely she was curious.

"No time for that now, Timothy," he said aloud. "The work of the father first. Must clean up your mess, Timothy."

Tim inhaled deeply on the cigarette, closing his eyes tightly.

***

10:21 p.m.

Fred completed his circle of the parking lot. Only two cars there and neither was Tim's Lexus. *Good*, Fred thought.

Time to set up. Fred turned and drove just past the alley on the adjacent street. One side of the street was under construction, and although closed at this hour, most of the small businesses down the block displayed signs that told people they were open during construction. Fred was glad for the location. There was not likely to be much traffic.

Fred pulled over and parked. He opened the console between the driver and passenger seat and took out the boot knife. It was custom made for him, weighted just slightly so that, with practice, most people would be capable of hitting their target with the blade at least ninety-five percent of the time. He normally ordered a dozen at a time, and this one was his second to last from the recent order. Only three had been used for assignments. He had dulled the blades of the other with practice and tossed them into the river. Although he knew well enough how to sharpen them, he preferred to use that talent for his kitchen knives. Chopping garlic was a task worth the time. Work tools were just work tools.

He checked the .380 and put it back in its holster. There was no way of knowing what might happen in the next forty-five minutes, but Fred was certain that some kind of ending was near. He was not restless, as he sometimes was with this kind of unexpected task. He was calm like he was with most normal assignments. But, more, he was tired. Sobriety seemed to bring something more with it. What he had been doing for the last thirty years was not okay, nor were any of the other practices the family engaged in. Not like some kind of movie where you turn on the family, Fred thought, but there was definitely no energy left for his work.

Fred tucked the knife in the slim holster on his belt and stepped out of the car. He stepped over to the large garbage dumpsters in the alley behind and just east of the building, which provided a clear view of the parking lot Tim was most likely to use. Unlike what most people thought, Fred was someone who had to know people, had to know what most people were likely to do in a given situation. Whatever Tim was up to, whatever kind of weird thoughts had driven him to be involved in things he didn't understand, he was likely to be as predictable as most in certain situations. Fred would wait. Tim would arrive at eleven, maybe a few minutes before or after. He would wait a few minutes in his car, and then he would go to the restaurant. Once he was out of his car, Fred thought, he would discover that he was in over his head.

***

10:23 p.m.

Mark watched as Tim entered the gas station and came quickly back out. He pulled into the parking lot for the convenience store kitty corner and around to the other side of it. He could see Tim standing and smoking, but Tim would not be able to see him. What was he doing in Melrose Park? Who was he meeting?

If Tim had been with Morgan and Bernstein at some time in his career, that meant he at least knew about the family and its business. It was possible he was kept on the outside, working at the firm but on its more legitimate side. *Possible, but not likely*, Mark thought. It made sense that he practiced the kind of law he did if he had been or still was associated with the family. What he might have had to do with Antoinette's disappearance was something Mark could not even imagine. Mark was glad his mind could not wrap around the kind of thinking it took to betray someone like Rachel by having anything to do with putting her sister even close to family business. Even if he was lining her up with

144

unbelievably wealthy contacts and contracts, it all had a darkness underneath that eventually crept to the surface.

"You should save that line," Mark joked to himself, "For that book you haven't written yet."

As Tim opened the door to his Lexus, Mark tried to shake off the unexpected mood shift the words had brought to him. Right now, preparing to drive himself into another dangerous setting, he felt odd about the work he told himself and his boys he did. He enjoyed his work as a private detective. He loved the puzzle and the sense of accomplishment when any type of case was resolved. Whether it was an adoption search, a criminal defense investigation, or even a background check, he felt good knowing that he had been able to provide a service for his clients and that he was responsible for providing that unique service.

As he started to drive back out onto the street, flipping on his left turn signal as Tim turned the corner, he remembered what Jason had said to him that day about a month ago when they were down at Wilmette Harbor perch fishing. *You should write stories about what you do, daddy. You tell good stories to Ian and I.* Mark did not correct him and say *Ian and me.* There was a time and place for that. Perch fishing was neither.

Tim's turn signal came on, and Mark slowed. Tim pulled into the parking lot next to a closed building. He pulled in, parked, and remained in his car. Mark circled the block and parked just past the lot. There was no way of knowing if Tim was waiting for someone, or if he would get out of his car and perhaps go to the all night diner just down the block. Mark knew he had to get out, though, and stay in the shadows. Anything could happen and happen quickly.

He opened his door, stepping out to the back of the car. His dome light was shut off so that he could open his car door without drawing attention, and he learned a long time ago that if he let his car door close on its own, it closed completely and with almost no sound. He quick-stepped across the street and walked between the two buildings that were adjacent to the west side of the parking lot. From behind the dumpsters, he could see Tim.

***

Mark watched as Tim stepped toward the alleyway, his calf length, wool coat discernable even in the poor light. Tim appeared to be looking for someone. His steps were slow and cautious, and his head moved around. He was anxious. Mark gripped the .45 and slid it out of its holster. He kept the barrel pointed down and slightly in front of him as he edged closer to the end of the dumpster.

A figure was approaching from the opposite side of the alley. Tall and muscular, his hand was in his jacket as if he were holding something inside it. Tim stopped and reached inside his coat. Mark stepped out from behind the dumpster without completely revealing himself.

"You and your kind that mock family. I knew you when you walked into the meeting, and I knew you didn't need a sponsor. You need punishment. You need to be shown the price for the error of your ways," Tim said, and, in what seemed like almost surreal slow motion, Mark saw Tim's hand move out from under his coat as he got close to the other figure. His hand moved up and forward, and though Mark could not see it, he was certain Tim was pointing a gun.

"Judge not," the other figure replied.

As Mark heard the pop of a small caliber, he saw the arm of the other figure complete an arc and watched as Tim grabbed for his throat and then fell forward. The figure had closed the distance to Tim quicker than Mark had anticipated, and his foot slid underneath Tim, rolling him over. Mark stepped out from the shadows just as the figure placed his foot over Tim's throat.

"You're a sick man," the tall figure said, and Mark saw his foot step down on an object protruding out of Tim's throat. "What you did to that girl was not right."

"She...she," Mark heard Tim's raspy, gurgling voice stammer, "was no better...than you."

The figure looked up at Mark and then away.

"All right, Fred. Step away from the body," Bob Tyse's voice called loudly.

Mark watched as Bob stepped out from the side of the building across from the parking lot. His revolver was drawn, pointed directly at the tall figure. Bob took a couple steps closer, and the figure turned to face him. Mark watched for the few seconds that seemed like an eternity. The tall figure stood silent, motionless.

"Detective Tyse," Fred replied and dropped his hands to his side. "Let me just say, it's an honor."

With quick, deliberate motion, the tall figure reached his right hand into his coat and drew out a weapon. He took one step forward, and his arm made a slight motion forward. He shot Tim once in the head and then turned back toward Bob. His right arm was back down at his side. He took a step toward Bob and raised his arm in a motion that seemed almost as if someone were pushing down on his firearm.

"You're leaving me no choice, Fred."

"I got your back, Bob," Mark shouted and stepped forward.

"Stay where you're at, little man," Fred shouted, his head turned slightly in Mark's direction but still facing Bob.

Mark looked at Bob and took a few steps closer.

"You're done, Fred. Lower the weapon."

"I am done, Detective Tyse. And I'm ready."

Mark watched as Fred's hand moved upward; then, he heard a shot and the crashing of glass. Mark squeezed the trigger twice on his .45 and heard the echoing of two other shots. Fred stood for a moment, motionless, and then fell backward. Mark's right hand dropped down, his .45 again pointed at the ground in front of him. His finger, by sheer muscle memory back off the trigger, aligned itself just above the trigger guard. He stood still for what seemed an impossibly long time before he realized Bob was already standing over the two bodies. Perhaps, Mark thought, he was done too.

"You okay, Mark?" Bob shouted.

"Yeah," Mark replied and looked at his right hand. His thumb moved to drop the magazine, and then he rocked the slide back, ejecting the round that had been chambered. "I'm not hurt."

"Okay. Good. If you don't have them with you, go get a cigarette. Take a few minutes at the car if you need to. The machinery will take over soon. That will include the press...can't keep you out of this one."

"Right," Mark responded and looked at Bob.

As long as he had known Bob, he wondered what it must have been like for Bob to be in Afghanistan, a marine sniper, his primary function to pull the trigger. He knew Bob as a family man, a man who ran for a children's charity, a man who helped people on the street as often as he arrested them. Now, Mark thought, it was easy to see why Bob worked as hard as he did to do as much as he could for people. Taking a life, even the one of someone who threatened you, did not have a simple sense of righteous finality.

Mark holstered his firearm and walked over to one of the parking blocks. He sat down, took out a cigarette, and lit it. He stared at the cigarette and thought of his regular joke about getting *organic cancer.* He closed his eyes tightly, and a picture of Jason and Ian, sitting by the campfire roasting marshmallows, appeared behind his eyes. He knew he was not about to quit smoking right now, but he felt it might be time to do so soon.

CHAPTER SIX

Two weeks later

"Jason," Mark said and stepped slightly to the side so Jason could shake the extended hand. "This is Rachel. Rachel, Jason."

"Hello, Rachel. I'm sorry for what happened to your sister. I mean, I didn't know her but..."

"It's okay, Jason," Rachel said and stooped down to look him in the eye. "I know what you meant. It's sad, but I'll remember her for all the good times we had. And it is a pleasure to meet you. I've seen pictures of you and your brother. Quite the brave explorers, you are."

"Thank you. You're really pretty. Did my dad tell you you're really pretty? Because I think you are, and he should really tell you."

"I'll consider him on notice, Jason. Did your dad tell you there are snacks in the other room? Sometimes grown-ups forget these things."

"Oh, he told me. But he said I should wait."

"Oh, dear," Rachel said, an exaggerated drawing in of her breath. "I didn't know he could be such a tough dad. You go ahead, Jason. Take Ian with you. I know there's a few other kids over there."

Jason looked up at Mark. Mark nodded, smiled, and tussled Jason's hair before he ran over to the other room, grabbing his younger brother by the arm and telling him about the snacks as they went. As they stepped into the adjacent room, Mark turned back to Rachel.

"It really was a nice service, Rachel. Wish I could have met her."

"Thanks, Mark. She was...a bright light."

"Well, Mark," Andre said and stepped up to hug Rachel. "Now that you're a famous private detective, will you be working only for the celebrity set?"

"Are you saying you can afford a bodyguard now, Andre?"

"Oooh, don't you tease."

"Is there anything you two want to tell me?" Rachel said.

They looked at each other, and their smiles turned to a gentle laugh. Mark looked at Rachel, openly admiring her smile. Their eyes met, and they both wondered the same thing for a moment: was it wrong to be thinking about being attracted to someone at this point in time, under these circumstances...or, maybe, was it time to allow and accept instead of trying to control? Andre noticed the pause after their eyes met and put an arm around each of them.

"So, three's a crowd. I told Drake I'd meet him after the service for a late lunch."

"Drake, Andre? What happened to Lucius?"

"Mark, believe it or don't, I think I actually listened to something Rachel had to say. Maybe the type you find yourself drawn to isn't the best type for you. You know, in a way it's kind of like an addiction thing. We all do it in different ways, you know...keep doing something 'cause it's easier than asking for the help we need to make some changes. I mean, it was sort of flattering that Lucius would get jealous, but then there was always trouble too. I don't mind a little drama now and then, but all the time? Lord, no."

"Hmmm," Mark replied, his mind immediately going to what Bob had said the other night about politicians, about people having behaviors that act just like addictions—

behaviors people chose to do compulsively that had a dangerous, self-destructive possibility if they went too deep. Religion, relationships, even charity work could become something to do just to focus on others, to avoid asking ourselves serious questions about who we are.

"Well, Andre," Rachel said. "So this is how I find out you're actually listening to me."

"Sometimes even I have to listen to my older sister."

"Now you better run, Andre," Mark said, holding up his arms in front of his face, feigning a protective stance.

"That's all right, Mark. I may be his older sister, but 'least I'm not old enough to be his father.'"

"Ouch. I'm going to leave before it gets physical. You know, my Rae, it might be time you looked at some things different too."

"I know, Andre. I guess I have to admit that my little brother can be right too. For now, though, have to just let it all be."

"Oh, Rae, I know that. Give me a hug...both of you."

Andre hugged both of them and walked away. They both watched him. Rachel hoped that Drake would treat him better than Lucius. Mark wondered if Andre ever felt his on-stage persona asked too much of him. Mark had worked undercover for almost four years and knew it could be a strain to pretend.

"So, what are you going to do next? Andre's right you know. You made headlines in both the *Trib* and the *Times*. You could capitalize on that."

"I'll leave that to the Bert Ratsos of the world—they love a headline. Rachel, I really think I might need to make some changes, take a little time."

"Me too. Been caught up in all the not-so-important things that people like to collect to make themselves feel important. Can't help but wonder if even Tim was more part of collecting the proper and practical, rather than listening to myself."

"Wow, that's a lot. I know I need to slow down a little. Listen to some of the people who tell me I should write."

"That sounds like good advice. I'm guessing those two little cuties in the snack room would like to have dad around more often."

"They love their mom time too. She is a good mom and a good person, even if she and I couldn't agree about a lot. I think she was just too used to being a single mom, making all the decisions, and didn't know how to be a partner...allow for someone to be an equal, trust that different doesn't always dictate better or worse."

"Sounds like you've given it some thought."

"After a year or two, you have to...have to make peace or completely separate for the kids' sake."

"Ah. So you have a plan then?"

"No, no I don't. And I guess, as much as anything else, it's probably time I started working on that. I've done okay for the most part winging it, but as Andre said, maybe it's time I looked at a few things differently."

"Like writing?"

"Could be."

"Well, it turns out I have a little extra money if you need to take a little time to go write that detective novel."

"Hmm. You know what they say Rachel: nothing's free."

"Well, I could use those warm hands of yours after I get through the next few days. When everyone's gone back to their lives, and I still have to pick up the pieces. Watching out for Annie was...a part of my life."

"That will take some time," Mark said and stepped over and behind her, placing his hands on her shoulders. "You want to be careful about trying to fill that space too quickly."

"You know," Rachel said, closing her eyes for a moment and allowing the warmth from Mark's hands and the strong but gentle pressure of their movement to take away some of the emotion trapped in her muscles. "Writing or maybe counseling."

"It's funny, private investigations can make you see a lot about people's behavior, a lot about what people do to themselves as well as each other."

"Well, I'm guessing not every private detective pays quite as much attention to people, really listening and thinking beyond the dollars and cents of it."

"Thank you, Rachel."

"Yeah, I could definitely use a massage like you started the other day. Maybe Saturday?"

"The boys are going to be with their mom all weekend—trip to Disneyworld."

"Not quite camping."

"No. But not a bad experience for them. She's not one for a lot of camping, but she does give them a variety of vacations—location and setting. Took them to the Badlands last year."

"Not sure how well I'd do sleeping on the ground either, Mark," Rachel said and put her hand on Mark's. "But, if you keep that up, I'll be asleep in a couple minutes. I'll probably need that come Saturday, but right now I have to go be with family as this winds to a close."

"Okay. Saturday should work, as long as I can order pizza."

"As long as you like sausage and heavy garlic."

"Well, can you work with green olives too?"

"I can."

"That should eliminate anyone kissing either one of us for at least twenty-four hours. Okay, let me round up those boys. You have a lot of people to say goodbye to."

Mark walked over to the room where the snacks were. As Jason had remarked, Rachel was beautiful. She was tough, too. But strong people needed support too. Rachel had been more like a mother for years, and it took control of her life in a way that kept that easier, much as he had buried himself in his work after the divorce. Weekends with the boys were great, and so were their summer camping trips. But they needed to see him happy more of the time. As he turned to look for the boys, Mark wondered if it was ever too late to wake up from a life created to avoid instead of engage.

EPILOGUE

"Hey, boss," Tony said, closing the door behind them as they walked into Michael's office on the 23rd floor of the LaSalle street building. "Why don't you do this at home?"

"Tony, Tony. One place I know I'm never alone is at home. Here, I can control plumbing, electric, phone, everything. Offices on this floor and the floor above and below are friends of the family...even in Rosemont or Riverside, you can't pick your neighbors as well. Now, get a drink or something if you want and then grab a seat. Going to put it on the big screen," Michael said and walked over to the cabinet across from his desk. "Vito," Michael clicked the power button on the remote as he turned to look at Vito. "Grab that dish of nuts on your way over."

"Okay, boss," Vito said and stepped over to the mahogany filing cabinet the dish rested on. He placed the dish on Michael's desk and stepped over to one of the high-backed office chairs next to Michael's. "You sure you don't want a drink, boss?"

"You know what, Vito? I think I will have one. I'll get it though."

Michael walked to the small kitchen that adjoined his office, bent down, and opened a small, locked door. He took out the bottle of Jack Daniel's Special Reserve and a low ball glass. He stepped to the mini-fridge, got a few ice cubes, and dropped them in the glass. He liked the tinkling sound they made on the glass. He filled the glass three-quarters high, put the bottle back in the cabinet, and locked it again. The Gentleman Jack standing next to the other liquors on the shelf above the mini-fridge was good enough for Tony and Vito.

"Now," Michael said, looking at his watch as he sat back in the chair behind his large office desk. "In about one minute, we'll be talking to Don Justino. Remember, he asked for you to be here, so no bullshit."

"You got it boss," Tony said and folded his arms over his chest, sitting back in his chair.

As Michael took a sip of his drink, a small line of text appeared across the large television, and Michael clicked to accept the call. For a brief few seconds, there was fuzz, and then a scrambled picture came into focus.

"Michael, how are you?" Don Justino asked from his couch.

An ornately carved coffee table stood in front of him, three small cups resting in front of each of the people assembled. Michael knew Vinnie. If you were ever granted an audience with Don Justino, or he demanded one of you, you met Vinnie. He was surprised to see a woman seated with them, and he had never seen her before. She wore a tightly-fitted black wrap dress, knee length, that while somewhat revealing in its neckline was nonetheless quite tasteful, a step up from business casual. Her chestnut brown hair was long, wavy, and worn so the left eye was slightly shielded from view.

"Don Justino, I am well. You look well."

"I am well. I like this...this skyping. I know you didn't always appreciate that I was fond of the old ways, but still you did as I asked. For this, I am grateful."

"Do you want to do anything about Tyse and this private detective?"

"We'd be happy to take care of those two," Vito interjected.

Michael turned quickly to Vito. His hand squeezed the arm of the chair, but he hesitated before saying anything.

"I was speaking with Michael, Vito. I want you there, Vito and Tony, because you are Michael's people and should know what we're talking about. But if I want your thoughts, I'll ask Michael for them. Now, Michael we are going to leave them alone. Two dead who are not going to be tied back to us. Tyse knows he has nothing, so all he can do is go back to his same work. We don't want to cause trouble for anyone. We like this mayor; he knows business. Private detectives we don't worry about...the worst he can do is write a book or a bad screenplay."

"So we'll keep the idea that the party was a going away party for you? And the girl was just someone we wanted working for one of our businesses?

"Very good, Michael. That's why I like you looking out for us: you are smart and quick. Of course, I am sad that Fred was not able to retire well for all his work. I liked Fred. Fred was like Sam—not just another simple, predictable soldier. He will be missed."

"I know he was someone you relied on," Michael said, not sure what to say but knowing he had to acknowledge Don Justino's feeling. "It was unfortunate. The lawyer?"

"Old business with Sam and best left in the past. Now, we look forward. I want you to meet someone. She'll be leaving for Chicago in two weeks. I want you to trust her as you trust me. She'll be working with you as a partner."

"A partner?"

"Yes, I know, it's not the old way. But, it is time. You two will work together, and no one will tell you what to do except Vinnie or me. The others still run their businesses as they need to, but I want the two of you to oversee, to make sure it all works together as parts of a whole."

"I am honored, Don Justino. Who is this lovely, young woman who rivals Giada De Laurentiis?"

"Very good, Michael. She is lovely, isn't she? But remember I don't put models with you as a partner. She knows how to use a knife or well-placed kick, as well how to use her curves and a whisper to get information. She speaks six languages and has her law degree from Eton. You need to remember always she is an equal."

"I will."

"Good. Michael, Amanda. Amanda Cesario, Michael DiNino."

"Cesario? Of the New York Cesario's?"

Amanda looked to the Don.

"Her father used to work for us, and when he retired he came back to the old country. He has brought his daughter up to take his position."

"Don Justino, I..."

"I know, Michael. It's hard to understand unless I tell you she carries her mother's name. Sam never got married. In his day, it was hard to do so with his job. And he wanted to protect her, so she has lived mostly on the islands."

"She's taking Fred's place?"

Michael heard an abbreviated chortle to his right and hoped it was not heard on the other end.

"They were supposed to meet at the party."

"I was upset to learn about Fred," Amanda said. "I would have liked to have met him. My father spoke highly of him."

"She will be doing much of Fred's work. But not in the old ways unless necessary. She will be a specialist to address some of our problems in a more contemporary fashion. Like you, Michael, she will use her education and related skills most often; she will work in plain view. Her work out of the public eye will be different than yours though."

"Don Justino has told me about you, Michael, and I look forward to working with you."

"I look forward to working with anyone who has gained Don Justino's respect and trust, Amanda."

Michael heard another muffled chortle and turned quickly. Vito's eyes looked away from his glare, and Michael turned back to the screen.

"Now, Michael, I have some business that needs my attention. When Amanda arrives, you help her find a place. Vito and Tony, remember Amanda works directly for me, just like Michael."

They both nodded.

"Michael, we will talk soon. Ciao."

"Buon giorno, Don Justino," he responded and waited to see the call was disconnected.

"You two," Michael said and reached over to grab a handful of nuts from the bowl on his desk. "You two are lucky because although you aggravate me at times, I want to enjoy that all this has been resolved. So, Vito, I have something for you."

Michael sat back in his chair and reached down to open the bottom right drawer. He looked at the cover of the movie case - Michael Keaton, Joe Picopo and Danny DeVito - and then at Vito and Tony. He knew he wasn't quite the character Michael Keaton portrayed in the movie, but he couldn't help but wonder if Vito and Tony weren't more like Joe Piscopo's character. They were more trustworthy, but, like the character, seemed to enjoy their work too much sometimes.and reached down to open the bottom right drawer.

He took out and placed a *Johnny Dangerously* DVD case on his desk, pushing it in Vito's direction.

"Put that in, and get me another drink, Vito. We'll see if we can help you enjoy the movie."

www.ingramcontent.com/pod-product-compliance
Lightning Source LLC
Chambersburg PA
CBHW070331130626
46556CB00007B/2800